LATE APEX

Jeremy DeConcini

ISBN: 197467911X
ISBN-13: 9781974679119

When a man is in despair, it means that he still believes in something.

—Dmitri Shostakovich

1

Skid Row, Los Angeles, California

Today was the day. He was on step 9. Making amends. He did not yet know the name of the human being he was going to make amends to, but he knew where he or she worked. He was done with the VA and their psycho drugs; he was done with the booze and the street drugs as well. Most of all, he was done with the violence. He left the men's shelter east of downtown, picking his way past the discarded needles and the hobo encampments on the sidewalk, and started the couple of miles to Union Station. He may have been a burned out drunk with a serious hitch in his step, but he had been a Ranger for nearly ten years. His fitness lingered; he could always tolerate a little hike. It was going to be a hot day in LA, but the shade of the high-rises was keeping downtown cool for the moment. He arrived at the art deco station and walked through the cavernous lobby and into the subway. He flinched and sped up his walk when someone asked for the time. He paid the fare and jumped on the newly created Expo line of the LA Metro system, which would take him to the west side.

Karl Steiger wasn't a particularly religious man, but he had been told by his sponsor that the 12 steps worked, and after what he had seen and done, that was good enough for Karl; he was out of choices. He was ordered into the AA program by the court as part of his sentence after nearly beating a guy to death at a biker bar in the valley, but despite the lack of choice in the matter, he was taking it seriously. He knew the path he had been on and where it led; he had to change. He also knew that his sins were too many and too varied to get forgiveness from each of those he had harmed, but if he could unload them all in a single confession, consequences be damned, then maybe he could start to forgive himself.

Karl's penance was due for the deeds he committed after he left the army to do virtually the same work for four times the pay with a security contractor in Iraq called Bear Claw Global Logistics. There was the family he was pretty sure he had clipped with his armored Tahoe at the head of his security convoy through Baghdad—a mother and her daughters—ended in a high-speed run through town. They weren't even in a particular hurry that day; it was just SOP to blast through town in the days after the war had supposedly ended, hauling ass, getting paid.

As the train clattered on toward Santa Monica through South Central LA, he watched the crowd change from working class and dark skinned to the white yuppie class of the west side as they got closer to the 405. The graffiti disappeared, and the cars got nicer. Macroeconomics in motion.

Karl had finished his career by trying to kill a graduate student who was trying to figure out where all the Colorado River water was going. He stalked her and her ex-FBI boyfriend all over the Southwest before taking a bullet to the pelvis for his trouble from the same ex-fed, who in retrospect had the same alcoholic, PTSD-addled, burned-out look he now recognized in the mirror every morning. That last gunfight had left his partner and their bosses dead and Karl on the run. He went to Mexico, then Thailand, then Indonesia. He eventually realized that nobody was looking for him; nobody cared what had happened. So he slinked back to the States and alcoholic oblivion. Until very recently, he had dragged his leg around Skid Row looking for drugs, booze, or even spray paint, but that was all over now.

He jumped off in Westwood with a handful of college students who were eyeing him suspiciously. He started the two-and-a-half-mile walk to his destination. The sun was higher now, the heat building. He was starting to sweat, but he wasn't nervous; he was elated. One way or another, he was going to leave his demons in that building. He hit the eleven thousand block of Wilshire Boulevard and paused. He looked up at the huge white building fronted with its magnificent flags. He felt a surge of righteousness as he took a deep breath and walked into the Los Angeles Field Office of the Federal Bureau of Investigation.

2

Iraqi Desert

Mohammed Qureshi walked out of his dusty tent at dawn and squinted as he surveyed the desert. A hot wind was already blowing. He avoided cities now when he could, preferring to stay away and stay mobile. He wasn't a Bedouin, but he embraced the nomadic desert lifestyle of the Bedu. He and his men were camped in the desert outside of Mosul. They were preparing to take the city back from the Iraqi government and their American Special Forces allies for the third time. It promised to be a spectacular fight. As he thought about the impending battle, a subordinate raced up in a stolen American Humvee with a roof-mounted .50 caliber. He hopped out of the driver's seat and presented the general with a printout of an e-mail message. Mohammed quickly scanned the message.

"*Jayid jiddaan*," he said, obviously pleased. The meeting in Italy was on. He wouldn't be fighting for Mosul this time.

3

Bear Claw Global Logistics Headquarters, Reston, Virginia

Eric Kaiser leaned back in his chair away from the television and prayed that the Lord would give him guidance. The United States seemed to be disengaging from the Middle East, and he needed to boost his company revenues. He had recently been funneling as much as he legally could into the presidential election, hoping for a win. Both candidates would likely support a "muscular foreign policy," but one would be much more likely to use his contractors to do America's dirty work abroad and thus fill Bear Claw's and Eric Kaiser's coffers just like the old days. He leaned forward to his computer and donated another $100,000 to the super PAC that supported his guy and that had absolutely no interest in honest participation in the democratic process, only winning the election. As a mercenary himself, he appreciated their singular purpose.

4

Underground Laboratory in ISIS Territory on the Border of Iraq and Syria

Mohammed sat at his desk in the bunker. He went over all his correspondence with his seller, reviewed the specs of the device he was buying, and checked his travel plans. He got up and went over to his safe. He dialed in the combination and swung open the heavy door. He looked inside, then, satisfied that the money was still there, put his nearly useless Iraqi passport on top of the pile of money, then pulled out his valid but fraudulently obtained Greek passport. He then closed the safe with a satisfying *whoosh*.

Mohammed Qureshi (Mo to his long dead friends) was a tall, handsome man in his early sixties with a full head of gray hair that was often obscured owing to the climatic and cultural wardrobe requirements of life in the Middle East. He had cut his teeth fighting the Iranians in the '80s as part of the Iran-Iraq war. He had seen shocking cruelty committed by both sides. This included the use of chemical weapons deployed by his army, which had been purchased from the Americans. Of course, aerosolized chemicals don't differentiate between uniforms and tend to go where the wind carries them, bringing death to friend, foe, and nonparticipating goatherd in equal measure. In those days, he tried not to dwell on it. Such were the exigencies of war. A Ba'athist out of career expediency, he was smart and rose quickly through the ranks of Saddam's army, ultimately making general. Within the convoluted confines of Saddam's Iraq, he tried to be an upstanding soldier with a solid moral code. He mostly succeeded, or as much as was realistic given that he was part of a dictator's army that routinely made political enemies disappear into holes in the desert never to return. He was a Muslim, but at that time not especially so, the secular nature of Saddam's Iraq not requiring more than a token appreciation for the Koran.

As soon as George Bush started saber rattling about weapons of mass destruction in Iraq, Mohammed knew war was coming. He would fight as his duty required; he also knew that Iraq would lose. Neither prospect bothered him. Dying in battle would be an honorable ending for the lifelong soldier. If he survived the war, he figured that with his command and his English-language ability learned at university, he would be assured of a good job with the new government. He envisioned Iraq becoming a new Japan or Germany, reborn out of war and fertilized with US dollars into a glorious society with a roaring economy. He had some ideas to stabilize the Mosul Dam that would cost billions and create hundreds of jobs for his men. He imagined that by the time he died an old man, his children and grandchildren could live a free and prosperous life in a new Iraq.

When Baghdad fell, Mohammed ordered his men to make camp outside the city and stand down until further notice. He contacted the highest-ranking US officer he could find and officially surrendered to him and reported for duty. The Americans, appearing to have no plan at all in this scenario, weren't sure what to do with him. It was almost as if they hadn't considered that when they won there would be a huge enemy army to deal with. He was kicked around from functionary to functionary within the Coalition Provisional Authority for days. Men and women in their twenties from Texas who didn't speak Arabic and seemingly knew little of the Middle East or how to build a functioning government and who had no interest in dealing with the general. He was getting reports that his men outside the city were growing restless, and they were still fully armed. He didn't need a PhD to understand the dynamics of that situation. It didn't take long for warriors with nothing to do to find trouble. By the time Mohammed got word that the Americans were de-Ba'athifying the Iraqi government and disbanding the army, it didn't really matter that much because by then all his soldiers had disappeared into the desert with their arms. There had been no Marshall Plan to rebuild Iraq into a peaceful economic powerhouse. In fact, as far as Mohammed could tell, there had been no plan at all.

As the country descended into chaos, just getting food and water became an issue. Mohammed, who was well known and still commanded respect, found himself at the head of a small militia of several hundred battle-hardened former Iraqi soldiers. He started fighting again. He fought the Americans and their Shia puppets in the new Iraqi Army. It seemed like he fought forever. Over the course of the next few years, Iraq descended further into civil war. During these years, the general's entire family was killed. Two of his sons died fighting at his side in the Second Battle of Fallujah. His wife and one of his daughters were killed by a drone strike, by mistake, its cargo bound for someone else. His last daughter and three grandchildren were run down by a convoy of private American military contractors speeding through the city in their black SUVs. He would never forget the name on the side of the trucks: Bear Claw Global Logistics.

His own moral decay accelerated as the Syrian civil war kicked off and it kept going with the rise of the so called Islamic State, sometimes known as ISIS. The fundamentalist Islamic beliefs of ISIS were so violent that even Al-Qaeda had disowned them. By the time the last of Mohammed's close relatives had left the planet, the general might as well have been dead himself. The one thing left in his burned-out husk of a psyche was hate. Hate for the Iraqi government, hate for the Americans, hate for the West and its endless lust for oil, hate for the goddamned Sykes-Picot Agreement. He even hated T. E. Lawrence and his bullshit pillars of wisdom. As ISIS grew up and the American presence drew down, ISIS capitalized on his hate, and Mohammed's militia was folded up into the fledgling movement. He didn't necessarily believe in their horrifically violent version of Islamic justice, but he couldn't argue with results, and he had long since given up caring about morality in the conventional sense.

ISIS management recognized Mohammed's obvious talent and motivation, and despite his lack of enthusiasm as one of Allah's warriors, it wasn't long before he regained his old rank as general. He commanded several thousand men in battles against myriad foes. They weren't always victorious, but his army always survived to fight another day. He was a true leader. It wasn't long before ISIS started looking for bigger things, and they thought the smart and fearless field commander's skills might be put to better use than commanding conventional armies in battle. He was tasked with their largest operation yet. The success of which would mean the permanent establishment of the caliphate. Mohammed was to lead the group dedicated to sourcing the materials for and building an arsenal of tactical nukes. One to detonate in a Western capital and the rest to hold as an explicit threat. If ISIS could kill a bunch of Americans in a cloud of radioactive ash, then perhaps the Western world would get out of the Middle East forever. They would have to get their oil elsewhere. ISIS set him up inside one of Saddam's old bunkers, complete with water, air filtration, and enough power to fabricate whatever might be needed to construct the bombs. They worked next to a fleet of Hussein-family, vintage exotic cars on flat tires that weren't worth the time and money to remove from the bunker. This job turned out to be right in Mohammed's wheelhouse. He wasn't laboring under any illusions that paradise awaited him upon his death, but he was happy to work with the religious whackos of ISIS if it meant kicking off the yoke of the West and restoring the Middle East for the Muslim Arabs.

5

FBI Field Office, Los Angeles, California

Special Agent Joanna Lundkvist reported for work at 8:00 a.m. like every other day. She didn't like Los Angeles. It wasn't even in her top ten choices of assignments, but as they say, "The needs of the service…" Still, she usually enjoyed her work, and she made the best of La-La Land. Her normal gig was money laundering, but this week she was the duty agent. This meant that the second-year FBI special agent dealt with all the callers and walk-ins who decided that today was the day they must speak with the FBI. Nobody liked being the duty agent, but it was a necessary evil, and it was certainly entertaining. There were thousands of freaks in LA who absolutely had to tell the FBI something. She was just setting up at the duty desk with her coffee when she got a page that Karl Steiger was in the lobby and wanted to confess to a crime. She took a look at the surveillance camera that monitored the lobby and got a look at Karl. He looked potentially dangerous, but no more so than most of the other psychos who came in off the street on any given day. Just to be sure, she grabbed another agent to watch the screen while she interviewed him.

She absorbed Karl's tale of a conspiracy between the drug cartels and former special operations guys to steal the Colorado River with bemused detachment. This story was going to kill it at the weekly happy hour in Westwood. She was dutifully taking notes, fully intending to dump them in the trash once he walked out the door, when Mr. Steiger mentioned an ex-FBI agent named Ben Adams. She stopped and looked at the camera above her.

She was too young to have known Special Agent Adams, but his story was legendary. He was a metaphor for every time the bureau screwed you somehow. The next time they did it, you were going to "pull an Adams." Which meant that you were going to sue the bastards for a few million and retire early. Most of the younger agents with the bureau didn't think he even existed. To them, Ben Adams was the creation myth for disgruntled federal employees. It seemed impossible that he was actually out there somewhere on a beach with a beer in his hand, laughing himself silly with seven figures of DOJ lawsuit money in his bank account. What the copy-room bravado left out was that while the legend was mostly true, Ben Adams had also gone to prison for five years for the killing of a DEA agent and got the millions only after he was let out of solitary confinement, and he was now an antisocial, alcoholic burnout living somewhere down in San Diego, his nights filled with horrors. It wasn't exactly the dream that got thrown around on bad days down at the FBI. SA Lundkvist knew these details because her supervisor used to work money laundering with Ben Adams in San Diego and was on the same surveillance at the other end of the street on the night Adams killed DEA special agent Nunez. Lundkvist sharpened her pencil and took down Karl's entire story. This was way out of her league and would have to get kicked up a level. When it was over, she told Mr. Steiger to wait. She went back to her desk and picked up the phone and called her boss.

6

Mohammed Qureshi staffed his weapons lab with the best and brightest of the ISIS conscripts. He had a team of scientists to design and assemble the devices, a team of ISIS operatives to buy the fissile material, and himself to get the high-tech pieces. He quickly learned the ins and outs of modern e-commerce as it related to international trade in weapons technology. He created an online persona to match his Greek passport and a front company ostensibly located in Italy. He learned everything he could about nuclear-fission devices and the international trade in weapons technology. One of the critical pieces they needed for their device was called a krytron. Sometimes called a nuclear trigger or a triggered spark gap, it was very hard to come by. Variations of this device are used in many normal products that require precisely timed events, even something as simple as a photocopier. The ones that Mohammed needed, however, were specifically designed and sold for detonating an atomic weapon. A krytron is a very high speed switch, absolutely essential for the critical timing required to detonate a nuclear weapon. It takes less than thirty nanoseconds from the time the switch is charged to complete the cycle. The timing is has to be perfect so that the explosive charges in the weapon detonate simultaneously so that supercriticality will be achieved and the weapon will detonate. The device was the keystone to the establishment of a permanent Islamic state. Without it, ISIS was just another fundamentalist movement in the Middle East.

Mohammed dispatched his subordinates to the darkest corners of the most corrupt former Soviet states to locate uranium 235 for their bombs. The Russians had lost enough fissile material over the years that just a few days of browsing the dark web turned up enough prospective leads in the Balkans and the 'stans that there should be no problem acquiring the uranium. The procurement of the triggers, however, was going to be tough. There were very few manufacturers, and the best were in the United States. This presented a challenge, but not an insurmountable one; it had been done before. In the '80s, the Israelis smuggled about eight hundred of them out of the United States with relative impunity.

Through his research, the old general learned that there were enough legitimate sales of weapons and military technology around the world originating in the United States that it might be possible to put together a deal that could go unnoticed in the torrent of money and arms fueling conflict around the world. He just needed the right partner. Mohammed also learned that the patchwork of US laws that regulated weapons sales had loopholes big enough to drive several hundred M1 Abrams tanks through. Mohammed used deliberately bad English when querying arms brokers so that if the conversation deteriorated when suggesting anything illegal, he could chalk up to poor language ability any misunderstanding on the topic. Both parties would just then laugh it off and go their separate ways. After a few months of researching every electronics firm he could find, Mohammed singled out the company he thought had the best chance of coming through for him. It was called H, J and J Electronics, and it was based in San Francisco. H, J and J made a large assortment of electronic devices primarily for the government and largely for military applications, including nuclear triggers. During his research, Mohammed learned that H, J and J was a firm in trouble. Through simple online searches of newspaper articles, he found out all he needed to make the approach. After the death of the founding partner, the company had been taken over by his only son, who by all accounts had been rather sloppy in his administration. This ultimately resulted in the firm losing all of its very lucrative defense contracts, and it was struggling to find new business. The stock was down 50 percent from last year. This was the opening. He sent H, J and J a request for a quote, and they responded. This could work.

7

San Francisco, California

Giancarlo Trentino woke up at 7:30 a.m. in the master bedroom of his Victorian manse in the high-dollar neighborhood of Pacific Heights, San Francisco. He was thirty years old, tall, thin, and handsome, with a mop of luxurious black hair and a mild hangover. He normally rolled out of bed whenever he wanted, but today, as CEO, he was to give a presentation to the rest of the stockholders of H, J and J Electronics. His new girlfriend lay naked, barely covered by the sheets, and still asleep. He eyed her appraisingly and was pleased. She stood out, even among his regular stream of spectacular conquests. Smoking hot and very athletic with just a hint of an edge, she was becoming his partner in crime. She was tough enough for the big-wall rock climbing he liked to do yet could look and act the part that high society required. Her intellect was clearly razor-sharp, yet she wanted to do all the same crazy things he liked. He smiled at his good fortune and walked out of the room.

In the kitchen he made himself some coffee and assembled the ingredients for a kale smoothie. Sophia strode purposefully over to the shower and left the door open. From the kitchen he could just see her through the open bedroom door. He moved aside the sixty-meter dynamic climbing rope and full rack of cams, nuts, and other rock-climbing gear dominating his kitchen table and choked down the smoothie while admiring her beauty through the glass. He then tapped out an e-mail on his phone, quickly swallowed his coffee, and went to the garage without saying goodbye. He strolled past his Ferrari, his vintage Land Cruiser, and two identical race-prepped BMW motorcycles to his prize, a 1933 Matchless Silver Hawk. A rare and expensive motorcycle, he had bought it at auction last year and loved it. He had some hot-rod guys he knew upgrade the engine and run it with straight pipes, much to the horror of the fundamentalist wing of the motorcycle-collecting world. It was antique, gorgeous, and fast as hell, made all the more fun and dangerous by its ancient design.

Moments later he blew out of the garage on the Matchless. He ripped through his neighborhood at high speed, the hammering of the V-4 engine banging off the walls of his neighbors' Victorian houses. He snapped it into second, and the rear tire barked its compliance. He loved antagonizing his uptight neighbors with his bike, but the truth was, in Pacific Heights, virtually all the homes were empty—fourth or fifth homes for the US oligarchy. He slid sideways past Larry Ellison's house, then did a big smoking donut in front of the statue with the cock and balls supposedly put up by one of Mr. Ellison's neighbors strictly to piss him off. Giancarlo took comfort in knowing that if anyone was indeed home in these houses, they would be rattled out of bed as he roared off. He mentally rehearsed his speech as he raced through town toward his office in the Tenderloin. He needed to hit all the traditional high points: history; technology; US military and technological dominance; clearer skies for H, J and J in the future; and so on. The truth was that he didn't give a shit about electronics and the long-term future for H, J and J, which was in serious jeopardy, but he had to keep up appearances so that when the music stopped, he would be certain to have a very comfortable chair.

Giancarlo entered the building through the main entrance on Golden Gate Avenue and into the large auditorium left over from when the building had been leased by a now defunct private university. He gingerly walked onstage to moderate applause. His father had been loved, and although Giancarlo wasn't his father, the shareholders still gave him superficial respect. He went through his speech to an anxious audience. The rumors had been going around: layoffs, factory closures, declining stock value. They needed a winner. There wasn't much substance to his speech, but Giancarlo sold it well. He went through the usual patriotic bluster that the defense industry practically invented. He hit a few of the high-tech products they were developing and that promised to save the company if the navy would only sign the contract. He assured them that this was due any day (it wasn't). That Congressman So-and-So was behind them 100 percent (he wasn't). By the time he was done, the audience might have actually believed it. They roared their applause as the "Star Spangled Banner" rose up and burst forth through the speakers at the end of his speech. Giancarlo made his way to the reception and glad-handed some of the bigger shareholders. He tried to rope a few of the younger guys into drinks at a strip club in Chinatown, but they begged off, claiming family obligations. That was fine with Giancarlo; they were dull anyway. Walking out of the meeting rooms, he checked his phone and saw Mohammed's confirmation. They were on.

When he had taken over his father's job at H, J and J three years before, it was obvious to all involved that Giancarlo was something of a fraud. His reputation as a hard-partying playboy with virtually no work ethic had preceded his takeover by about ten years. His father had come from nothing and had spoiled his only son, particularly after his wife died. Giancarlo grew up to be a walking, talking, drug-addicted argument in favor of a high estate tax. Things started going south for H, J and J pretty fast after Ettore's death and Giancarlo's takeover. It wasn't entirely his fault: Giancarlo's father and H, J and J management had no succession plan in place. Ettore Trentino, like so many hard-driving, self-made men, had simply assumed he was going to live forever. The combination of instability in the company and Giancarlo's reputation was enough for the government to seek out new suppliers of high-tech war-making devices. Giancarlo was trying to figure out new revenue streams when he saw Mohammed's RFQ.

8

Fort Meade, Maryland

Giancarlo's e-mail pinged off a server in Iraq, which sent a little electronic notice deep underground in the bowels of Fort Meade. The notice made the sound of a shotgun loading a shell from Ed Forrester's computer. He wheeled his chair over to check it out. Ed was midforties, slightly pudgy, with skin the color of someone who spends his working life in a basement. Like a lot of young men in America, Ed had wanted to serve his country in some way. He wasn't tough enough for the military, and it turned out he had smoked way too much weed at Boston College studying computer science for the FBI to consider him, so after graduation he took a job with the NSA in one of their newly created, post-9/11, Cheney-sanctioned Dark Side programs. Ed's narcotics background was less of a concern to the NSA given the probable unconstitutionality of the programs. His very existence was going to be so secret that it didn't matter how many times Ed had "healed the nation" in his dorm room in the '90s listening to Peter Tosh. Though whistleblowers ultimately informed the public about many of the surveillance programs, it turned out that the public actually didn't care. So long as nothing exploded at the hands of somebody allied to Islam, the people gave the government free rein to spy on them. The hiring practices eventually tightened up at the NSA, but Ed was good at his job and hadn't become a liability, so he stayed.

This type of thing was normally out of his range, but since the e-mail had pinged off a known ISIS server, Ed had been tracking him. Besides the server hit, the factor that raised a red flag was the sheer number of switches Mohammed was trying to purchase. Six for a hospital in Peshawar on a letter of credit might have been legit, or it might not have been, but the four hundred Mohammed was negotiating at $2,000 apiece cash in person could mean only one thing.

Ed had informed his supervisors when he saw the original e-mail and was told not to act but to continue monitoring the situation. He was not to let any other intelligence agencies know, and most important, under no circumstances was he to let anyone in law enforcement know; those guys screwed up everything. Ed was annoyed at the instruction, and though he wasn't particularly patriotic, it seemed to him that his job existed specifically to keep people like ISIS from getting things like nuclear triggers. Ed assumed that management was going to power play the situation to emotionally blackmail Congress for more money for some new, extralegal surveillance program.

He couldn't let it lie, but he also didn't want to do anything that would jam him up with his superiors. He had already gotten a warning from management for blasting Judas Priest too loudly in the basement. There was a guy who lived in his building near Georgetown who might be able to help.

9

San Diego, California

Ben woke up around seven and wandered naked to his kitchen. He was in his upper thirties now and slightly taller than average, and he was still fit despite the booze, his body whittled down by the ocean to pure purpose. He went to work crafting a caffe latte with his inappropriately elaborate espresso machine. Geronimo poked his leg to indicate a lack of food and water. Ben sorted him out with some dry dog food and cooked ground turkey, which pleased Geronimo greatly. He got dressed, and he and G-dog walked down his street to the beach and wandered out along the cliffs to check the waves, as was his habit. There was supposed to be a new swell filling in, but it wasn't showing yet. He wandered up into La Jolla where he bought another coffee at The Roasters and checked the reefs. Same story: no swell yet. He ambled down Dolphin Place and knocked on a familiar door.

New Zealand hadn't worked out for Ben. Jessica was perfect, and Raglan was perfect; it was Ben who was bent. Even in paradise, where his only worries were what fish were biting and when the next swell would arrive, the psychic pressure of having to share his life with someone else was too much. The drinking got heavier, and he became prone to unprovoked anger. He got into a brawl with a Maori guy in town for no reason and got stomped for his trouble. He had to leave. He took Geronimo and retreated to his tattered apartment in Pacific Beach, one of the rougher coastal neighborhoods of San Diego. Back to the beach with his crusty neighbors, one step from homeless guys who spent their days self-medicating with surf, alcohol, drugs, or all three. He was back with his people.

He justified his leaving Raglan in part by telling himself that Jessica was better off without him, and although he was probably right, she would have disagreed had she been given the chance. He felt better back in San Diego, where he could crawl back into his solitary head space with his demons and his dog. They all shared his crappy apartment near the beach with his worn-out hand-me-down furniture and cheap decorations. Geronimo seemed to still hold a grudge about the length of the plane flight from New Zealand and possibly was indignant on Jessica's behalf, but all was otherwise OK in his world. Ben liked San Diego; it didn't change much, and its gritty edge seemed to suit Ben just a little better, a more accurate reflection of himself than an unspoiled Aotearoa was. The beaches, palm trees, and broken misfits he hung out with were all still there in Pacific Beach. Phil the conspiracy theorist was still smoking weed and cruising from surf spot to surf spot in his worthless van filled with priceless surfboards and telling anyone who would listen about the latest sinister conspiracy that the media didn't want you to know about. Another fixture of the surf scene in Pacific Beach and La Jolla, Bob the veterinarian/weed dealer was still around. He lived on the cliffs of La Jolla and had a history of military action in Afghanistan related to the army's dogs. They were all just as Ben had left them twelve months ago. It was Bob Kreiderman's door that he was knocking on now.

The vet/vet answered the door in board shorts with his own coffee.

"What's up, man? Good to see you. Come on in," he said, welcoming Ben into the foyer and giving Geronimo a treat as he blew past and onto the patio to chase a seagull.

"Man, I forgot how good your view is here," said Ben, looking straight down onto South Bird Rock, one of the better reef breaks in the area. He hadn't been inside this house in almost two years. Bob looked over his shoulder at his multimillion-dollar view.

"Yeah, it's pretty sweet."

"No wonder you get so much good surf: you know the moment the waves turn on," Ben kept on without inflection.

"A healthy dose of natural talent is helpful in that regard," Bob said, smiling.

Ben gave him the middle finger, recognizing that the conversation was rapidly deteriorating.

"What did you want me to look at?" Ben asked.

"The State of California is considering legalizing weed, and I want you to look at the proposed law and see how hard it would be to get into it if I decided to go that route."

Bob had made the money to buy his oceanfront surf palace not by practicing animal medicine but by supplying most of the beach towns between Encinitas and Imperial Beach with high-grade, provenance-proven California marijuana.

Ben laughed. "After all these years, you're thinking of going straight?"

"If this goes through, my cash flow is hosed, and there aren't enough cases of kennel cough in the world to pay the property taxes on this place, so if you can't beat 'em, well, you know…which reminds me…" Bob threw Ben a small box of flea-and-tick medication from his cabinet.

"OK, thanks. Throw it on my tab." Ben picked up a sheaf of papers from the coffee table.

Technically Ben was a lawyer. He had been to law school and had passed the bar exam in California, and he was in good standing with the committee. He even had business cards that said, "Ben Adams, Esq. Attorney at Law." But he didn't have an office, and he didn't have a paralegal. He didn't even have the obligatory black BMW 5 Series that is part of the SoCal lawyer uniform. He charged his weirdo friends and clients twenty-three dollars an hour to perform their odd legal requests. Working out of his apartment, he would appeal parking-ticket vehicle impoundments, do consultations on community-property law for the soon-to-be divorced, and apparently review pending legislation for drug dealers going legit.

Ben leafed through the statute on Bob's couch as Bob put a splash of scotch in Ben's coffee. Ben raised his glass to Bob and set it back down. He looked around the room at the framed photos from parts unknown of Bob and a bunch of what looked to be Special Forces operators with dogs. Bob had worked as a veterinarian for the army in the various US wars of the early 2000s. That background came in handy when, two years ago, Ben and Jessica had each been in need of emergency treatment for a gunshot wound apiece. It was the type of situation where a hospital visit and its attendant consequences just wouldn't do. Bob was a pro at battlefield medicine on both humans and animals, and he had sewn Ben and Jessica up on his kitchen counter and sent them on their way while keeping his mouth shut. He was that kind of guy.

Ben looked around the house, remembering his last blood-soaked visit, and noticed the efficiency of the place. Ben had known and surfed with the vet for ten years, and this was the first time he had really noticed that he moved and acted a lot like the Spec Ops and SWAT guys Ben had known over his years in government. In the lineup in PB or La Jolla, he had just seemed like another surfer in a black wet suit. As he thought back on that, he glanced out at the ocean and thought he saw a set start to stand up on the reef. It rolled over without quite breaking, just a big lump. It was supposed to be an El Niño year.

Where are the waves?

10

Golden Nugget Hotel Casino, Las Vegas, Nevada

He squinted as the dials spun in their electronic dance. Lemon. Lemon. Bar. The machine sang as the digital counter went up a few dozen clicks. He wasn't a gambler by nature, but he felt a trace of a thrill. That the amount he had just won was fifteen dollars didn't matter. It cut the anxious boredom. He looked up over the rows of slot machines. He saw them, playing roulette, laughing it up as the big wheel spun around. It all looked stable. He ordered another Coke from the waitress and spun the slot machine again.

He was Special Agent Howard Goodman (Howie to a very select group) with Homeland Security Investigations, based out of the DC Field Office. He was in his early forties and from New York, possessing a square build with a face that was neither handsome nor ugly. He looked like everyman, but an everyman whom no man messed with. His dad had been NYPD, and he had admired him greatly. He had wanted to follow in his footsteps and go NYPD since he was a kid, but his dad had pushed hard for his son to excel in school, not wanting him to endure what he had. Howard did well; he even made it to Dartmouth. He never did join the NYPD, to his dad's pleasure, but he threaded the needle by becoming a special agent with Homeland Security Investigations. His specialty was complex investigations related to counter-proliferation of weapons and weapons technologies, working exclusively undercover operations. He was in Vegas on a job. He was the case agent this time and the one person ultimately responsible if things went bad, but he needn't worry: this deal hinged on his regular undercover, Matt.

The man was gifted. He could pretend to be the shadiest arms dealer on the planet, go halfway around the world to Thailand during a coup, make the deal while the social order fell apart around him, go through the charade of getting arrested, and still go home and help with dinner and the kid's homework when he got back. At the moment, Matt was playing roulette with their target, a guy from Arizona who specialized in "hard-to-find aircraft parts." This was code; everybody knew what he bought and sold. For many years, there were only two militaries in the world that flew the Grumman F-14 Tomcat: the US Navy and the Iranian air force. Now there was only one. Back before the revolution, when the United States and Iran's CIA-installed leader, the Shah, were all still friends, the Iranians bought at least eighty F-14s. Now, with Iran under embargo from the United States, parts to keep those things in the air were very hard to come by. Luckily for them the US Navy had recently stopped using the planes and had started liquidating all their F-14s and associated parts. The Defense Logistics Agency, which conducted the fighter-plane yard sale, turned a blind eye to the fact that the only people who would try to buy F-14 parts, outside of a small group of very enthusiastic fans of the film *Top Gun*, would be the Iranian air force.

In the layers of laws making up the structure of US export policy, this would seem to be a rather large loophole. It was legal for the DLA to sell the parts in the United States; however, it was illegal to export them without a license granted by the State Department (which would never be granted to Iran if one were to apply). That the parts were all ultimately destined there was of no legal relevance. That as a policy prescription it would make much more sense to just destroy the parts and save the Department of Homeland Security the time and trouble of paying highly trained and motivated special agents to intercept them was apparently lost on the powers that be. It wasn't lost on Goodman, but he loved his job, and he didn't write the laws, so he let it ride.

All he had to do now was make sure Matt didn't get killed. He had a team of other special agents throughout the casino posing as patrons with the same objective: keep the undercover alive. How the Golden Nugget security hadn't hassled them yet, Howard had no idea. They had been there for hours drinking soda and dropping the absolute minimum into the slot machines. Either his team was just that good at blending in that casino security, with their thousands of cameras, hadn't noticed their op yet, or they stuck out so badly as feds that security knew what they were up to and were ignoring them. He very much hoped it was the former. Maybe they scrutinized only the people who were actually gambling. Either way, it was going smoothly, and they were almost home free. They had completed the deal nearly two hours ago in one of the hotel rooms upstairs. The CIA had provided them some very slick lamps with inboard cameras and mics, which they had installed in the room beforehand. It was a cash deal for a laundry list of parts for the Tomcat, including a hard-to-come-by and in good-condition cockpit canopy, which was in the hotel parking garage under a tarp at the moment. Matt posed as a straw buyer for the Iranians, and they had it all on tape. There would be no arrest tonight as they were still building their case, so they just had to keep gambling with the target until he got tired and they could call it a day. They would do a few more similar deals over the next few months and then take him down at once with overwhelming evidence and a bulletproof indictment.

After another hour and three more Cokes, it looked to be wrapping up. Goodman saw the undercover and the target migrate over to the cashier. He cashed out his slot machine, ending the evening up ten dollars, his hands starting to twitch from sugar and caffeine. The team shadowed both men to the elevators where, when it arrived, Matt begged off, claiming business at the front desk to avoid riding solo with the target. The debriefing occurred ten minutes later in Goodman's hotel room. Perfect op. They were back in DC the following day for the mounds of paperwork that follow every operation and followed up with a celebratory night of boozing at Chief Ike's Mambo Room.

11

Capitol Hill, Washington, DC

Ed the spy wasn't exactly friends with Goodman, but they were friendly enough in the hallway or the laundry room of their apartment building in Georgetown. Each had enough access to government computer systems that despite the NSA's reputation as "No Such Agency," Howard knew exactly whom Ed worked for and vice versa. Ed also knew from illegally pinging Howard's cell phone that he was at Kelly's Irish Times on Capitol Hill at this very moment. He cruised down there to see what the veteran investigator might think about four hundred triggered spark gaps headed into ISIS territory.

He saw Special Agent Goodman at the end of the bar chatting up what appeared to be some fresh Capitol Hill interns. In the background, the usual Tuesday-night band was into a full-tilt rendition of

"The Irish Rover." Ed walked up to him and got a beer.

"Ed, what's up?" Goodman smiled, pleasantly surprised. Before Ed could answer, he nodded to the attractive young blonde next to him. "Do you know Noreen? She works for Senator Rinehart from Wisconsin."

"Nice to meet you," Ed replied, raising his glass to the girl.

"And this," Howie said, indicating the equally attractive brunette on his other side, "is Barbara from Congressman Vitale's office. She and the congressman are both from New Jersey."

Ed raised his glass to her as well, noticing that both girls quickly and correctly assumed his place in the Capitol Hill power structure, then dismissed him out of hand accordingly. It also could just have been the mullet. Howie didn't have the Capitol Hill juice of a congressman, but he had a badge and a gun, and that went a long way with the ladies, Ed noted ruefully.

Ed quickly finished his beer and handed Goodman a manila folder.

"I wasn't here, and you don't know me," he said and walked away.

Intrigued, Howie Goodman opened up the folder on the bar, ignoring his buxom companions for the moment. He looked upon a single sheet of paper full of single-spaced text. It appeared to have been written in MS Word or some equally innocuous and untraceable application, and it detailed what Ed had learned about the upcoming deal for the nuclear triggers. The nature of the narrative obscured how the information had come to be known, although it was pretty obvious to Howie. The printout had no indicia of origin. It wasn't an ICM printout; it didn't come out of a State Department system. It might as well have been fiction to anybody else. But this was what Special Agent Goodman did for a living, and although he was just a Street Thirteen at work, he was quite good at it, and what he had in front of him was enough to start the kind of case that could make his career. He pounded his Jameson, kissed each girl on the cheek, and made his way toward the door. He tipped the band generously on the way out and stepped into the chilly Washington, DC, night. He was headed for his office. He had work to do.

12

Pacific Beach, San Diego, California

A t first Ben didn't let the lack of surf get him down. He used the time to go through his gear and make sure it was all in working order. He repaired the dings on his surfboards, replaced the line on his fishing reels, and oiled the mechanisms. He then replaced every fluid in the jeep, rotated the tires, and got underneath and scoured off any rust starting to form and repainted each spot. That took about a week. When the ocean remained flat, he started running with Geronimo on the beach. The dog seemed to enjoy the exercise, if not the leash. First, they ran three miles, then five miles. At ten miles Ben's knees and his dog started reminding him that he hadn't run regularly since the FBI academy over fifteen years ago. He switched from running to nighttime lobster diving in La Jolla and did a little spearfishing during the day.

He tweaked his taco recipes to fit what he had caught, really getting into the minutiae of what makes a good taco sauce. By the time he found himself analyzing historical weather data related to El Niño events going back sixty years, and correlating it to boom pepper producing years, he knew he was starting to break. He spent the next two weeks hammered at London's West End, a dive bar nearby full of misfits just like him.

Late one night, after a day of boozing at the West End, he came home and checked the weather maps. A big low-pressure system was forming off the Aleutian Islands. It was too soon to tell, but he thought it might have been the opening salvo of a big El Niño run of swell. He blacked out strung out yet hopeful.

13

HSI Field Office, Washington, DC

HSI special agent Howard Goodman spent the next two days confirming as many details of the document as he legally could. He was bound in ways that spooks at the NSA weren't, so he hammered down every detail that he could using his systems, commercial databases, and open-source intel. When he was done, he sat back and appraised it. At a brush, it was a perfect case. It had terrorism, corruption, greed, and some potentially prosecutable subjects. Best of all, this deal was imminent. Normally, to cultivate this type of investigation took months if not years. This was handed to him on a silver platter, and it was going down in sixty days. He would cover up the spy tracks and get the investigation backstopped from his end, and he would be good to go for prosecution. Howie would need to work fast to get an undercover in place. For this to work, he would have to learn his target's weak points, and he needed to find an under-cover agent with the chops to make the approach.

It wasn't hard to find out what kind of person the new CEO of H, J and J Electronics was as he wasn't exactly press averse. SA Goodman's first thought was to get a female agent in close to him, but he quickly dismissed that idea. HSI had some stellar undercover female agents and some great-looking ones as well, but unfortunately the ethical issues added up quickly in that scenario. Goodman was many things, but he wasn't about to add pimp to his résumé. He would have to come up with something else.

In a normal undercover investigation, the good guys would pose as either the buyer or seller, then ar-rest the bad guys who were working the other side of the deal. In this case, both the buyer and seller were the bad guys, and they were setting up the deal them-selves. Howie would get them both if he could find out where and when it was going down. The lovely side ef-fect was that it would also preclude any of the usual bullshit entrapment defenses that could be expected from the defense attorneys. Even better, the bad guys would likely each be so suspicious of the other that the possible presence of an unrelated UC agent might would not even be on their radar.

Digging deeper into Giancarlo Trentino's back-ground, he discovered a string of A-list girlfriends, fast cars, and a reckless lifestyle. He distilled his angle down to two interesting and seemingly unrelated parts: 1) that he was an only child and 2) that he was an aspiring motorcycle racer, with a race planned in South Africa in a few months. Employing a measure of armchair psychology, SA Goodman noted that the guys he had known growing up who didn't have siblings always seemed more inclined to yearn for that intimate competition and camaraderie that exists among brothers. He figured he might be able to use that angle to gain access to Giancarlo. According to Giancarlo's Facebook page, he had enrolled in a high-dollar motorcycle-racing school at Laguna Seca near Monterrey, California, hoping to hone his riding skills before the race in South Africa. This was his in. If he could insert someone into this school to befriend his target, he might get close enough to learn when and where this deal was going down. He wrote up and sent his memo requesting approval and funds for his operation. It would take someone pretty reckless to be the undercover in a motorcycle race. Goodman sure as hell wasn't going to do it.

14

San Diego, California

Ben watched the low-pressure system with anticipation. The entire surf community from Ensenada to Santa Barbara was on edge, and the tension was seeping into everyday life. People on the street were a little less friendly, and the traffic was a little more aggressive (if such a thing were possible in Southern California). But the storm was giving them hope. Ben checked the weather reports and buoy data hourly. The storm system was huge and growing, with sustained winds of ninety miles per hour and fifty-foot seas. But Ben noticed a problem: the storm was moving. Ideally the system would sit in the North Pacific and pound on it like a giant bass drum, sending waves south, but this one was headed down the coast, fast. It was currently tracking south off British Colombia and pointing stateside. Ben's hope diminished a bit, but he still held on to some that it would crash into a high-pressure system over the western United States and stall or, failing that, would slow down enough that he could catch a few of the front-runners of the swell before the impact of the storm hit San Diego.

15

Washington, DC

Somewhat to his surprise, Howard Goodman's operation was approved. His group supervisor was not afraid of taking risks to make big cases. There was one particularly large caveat, however: the undercover could not be an HSI agent. They weren't willing to risk one of their agents on a motorcycle after last year's four-wheeler accident along the California-Mexico border. An agent had crippled himself during a high-speed drug interdiction in the sand dunes, so the undercover would have to be someone from another agency or, failing that, possibly a civilian informant. This was bad news, but Howie knew that the way to eat an elephant was one bite at a time, and just getting the approval constituted a pretty big bite. Everything else could be worked out.

16

Reston, Virginia

Eric Kaiser was feeling good. The latest polls showed the election as a toss-up, but they were wrong: his guy was going to win. The government dollars would start flowing. Bear Claw was coming back. He could feel it. He watched the talking heads go through their shtick on television as he pounded out the miles on the treadmill at his private gym in Bear Claw HQ. He was going for five miles at a seven-minute pace, an easy workout for the former marine, just something to knock out before lunch. His phone pinged an e-mail just as he turned mile four. It was someone from his church group who also worked at FBI Headquarters. The e-mail had no subject in the heading and a single attachment. Kaiser opened it to see a smiling Karl Steiger sitting in the lobby of what was clearly some sort of government building. Eric knew this was trouble, but it was the kind of trouble he didn't mind dealing with. He loved having enemies. This would be a good distraction.

17

Georgetown, Washington, DC

At his apartment that night, Goodman racked his brain trying to come up with the right person for this case. He was digging around the bottom of the barrel when he remembered an old friend from college who had become an FBI agent and worked the West Coast. He thought he might have a line on a good UC operative in California who could pull this together. After some doing, he tracked down Joe Lanahan in the FBI attaché office in Puerto Vallarta, Mexico. He wondered aloud how many asses Joe had had to kiss to get that gig as he dialed his telephone number.

"Lanahan," the voice answered.

"Joe, it's Howard Goodman, from Dartmouth. How are ya?"

"Fucking great, man. How the hell are you? How is the Customs Service?"

"There ain't been a Customs Service since 2003, you jackass, but Homeland Security Investigations is fine. Thanks for asking."

"Good to hear it. Are you coming to Puerto Vallarta?" Howie heard a seagull squawk through the receiver past the voice of his old friend.

"Negative, bro, but I need your help with something."

"OK, lay it on me."

Special Agent Goodman proceeded to lay out the entire story for the FBI man, omitting nothing.

"Well, what do you think? Do you know anybody who could handle this?" he asked.

Lanahan took a long breath and said, "First, this is big balls, my friend. I have to give you that. I mean, this could go wrong a hundred different ways. You are really hanging it out there, man. Bravo."

"Yeah, yeah, who do you got?"

"I might know a guy."

"Cool. Is he FBI?"

"Not exactly," Lanahan said, exhaling deeply.

18

San Diego, California

Whatever it was going to be, today was it. Ben got up, for once without a hangover. He was starved for waves, and he wasn't going to blow it today. The swell was supposed to show up by midmorning, and unfortunately, the weather was showing up with it. He didn't care. It was going to be big, and he couldn't be choosy. He got up, made some coffee, and walked down to the beach. The wind had already begun to howl. He could see the swell starting to stand up on the reef, but the ocean surface was already whitecapping. He sat on the bluff for a while, Geronimo snooting around the grass and ice plants. Occasionally, a big lump would roll over the reef but not quite break. Geronimo took off after another dog that he knew, and Ben let him go. This was their turf. After about thirty minutes, Ben saw it. The horizon moved up just a bit. It was coming in, and Ben knew even before it hit the spot that it would be huge. No one else was out yet, so it was a little hard to predict where it was going to break. When it finally did, it exploded thirty yards farther out from the normal take-off zone. It was easily double overhead, maybe triple, and the swell was still building.

19

Los Angeles, California

The FBI gossip train ran quickly through the ranks. Those still with the bureau remembered the sting of that lawsuit and the attendant bad publicity it had brought down on the FBI. Forever conscious of its image, the bureau did not like admitting wrongdoing. When word got to the headquarters level that they could potentially put Ben Adams back in jail, there was muted celebration. They wouldn't get their money back, but there would be some level of vindication that he was indeed a "bad guy" and that they had been right to can him and send him to jail in the first place. That the bureau might in some way be responsible for how he had turned out and possibly the events they were going to pin on him now didn't even register.

At about the same time that the LA Field Office got the OK to work up an indictment on Ben Adams, the special agent in charge of the DC Field Office of Homeland Security Investigations was making a call to FBI Headquarters with an official request for assistance in procuring an undercover operative for the H, J and J Electronics smuggling case and that the operative be the same former FBI agent they were just about to jail. HSI didn't yet know the bureau had Adams over a barrel; they were just looking to sweet-talk him into helping with a nudge from a sister agency. When the higher-ups at each agency finally connected the dots, they knew they owned him. The FBI was reluctant to let Adams off the hook, but they figured this deal would work out in their favor. The op was so bat-shit crazy that it had to fail, and they would get to put Adams in the can anyway and watch Homeland Security embarrass themselves in the process. Win-win.

20

Ben whistled for his dog and took off for home. He knew he didn't need to run but couldn't help jogging. The little dopamine receptors in his brain that responded to surf had dried up a long time ago. He needed this. By the time he got home, the rain was coming down, and the wind was blowing a gale. Ben was still undeterred; he was going out. He pushed open the door to his single-story '50s-era apartment and went straight for his garage, where his boards and wetsuits lay perfectly organized and ready for duty. He didn't bother to turn on the lights in the apartment. He was almost to the garage door when Geronimo's growling stopped him. On his couch sat three figures in the darkness.

Ben immediately went for the gun on his hip that hadn't been there since he had left the FBI over a decade before. He shook his head at himself and said, "What the fuck do you guys want?"

Joe Lanahan turned on a light. "What's up, buddy? How about getting some coffee going?"

Ben was in no hurry to hear how his life was about to be fucked, so he wandered to the kitchen and got to work on the coffee. He watched as the gold Pavoni machine started to steam and gurgle, and he took a second's pleasure in the experience. He dropped the coffee hard on the table and went for a beer for himself. Aptly titled "Victory at Sea," it was an imperial stout with 10 percent alcohol content. It went with the weather, and Ben figured he was going to need it.

"What are you doing back in San Diego, man. Did they boot you from Mexico? Persona non grata?" Ben asked his old friend Joe.

"No, man. PV is still great. They brought me up here special just to talk to you."

"Jesus," Ben said past the bottle, then drank deeply. It was the bald guy's turn to speak.

"My name is Howard Goodman, and I work for DHS, HSI back east, in counter-proliferations investigations, and I have an important case I'm working that needs someone like you. Joe was kind enough to offer to make an introduction after he told me about the freelance job that you did for the bureau last year in Colorado. Everyone is still talking about what stellar work you did helping out on that case," he lied.

"What do you mean, *important*?" Ben asked, squinting.

"Like ISIS getting their hands on nuclear weapons important," Goodman said, looking him dead in the eye.

Ben looked the HSI agent up and down. He was reasonably fit for a guy pushing forty. His head was shaved, but for no apparent reason, Ben got the impression that if he let it grow, it would sprout a bush like Larry Fine from The Three Stooges. Somehow that made him feel better.

"So what do you need, and what's in it for me?" Ben asked, about halfway through his beer.

"We need you to get close to a trustafarian adrenaline junkie who is trying to sell a bunch of triggered spark gaps to ISIS so that they can build a nuclear weapon. Then tell us when and where the deal is going to go down. Simple and probably right up your alley," Howie said.

"Simple, huh? How exactly am I supposed to get close to this guy?"

"Time is an issue here, Ben, and we think our best chance is for you to enroll in the same motorcycle-racing school as him next week in Monterrey. Our target is an amateur road racer. Can you ride a motorcycle?"

"Of course I can."

Both of the other agents looked at their shoes for a second.

"What do you mean, motorcycle school? How did you get this lead, anyway?"

"Spook I know in DC gave it to me." Said Goodman.

"That sounds great. And how exactly do you expect that to hold up in court? It has been a while since law school; have they repealed the Fourth Amendment?" Ben asked, starting to fidget.

"Our priority is to disrupt the shipment. Prosecution is secondary. Besides, I can backstop the whole thing through non-classified open sources. It would probably hold up for an indictment," said the East Coaster.

"OK, fine. We still haven't gotten to why I would do this."

The third figure on the couch leaned forward to introduce herself—blond, petite, in her midforties with a severe look, but not unattractive.

"I'm Assistant United States Attorney Megan Campos. It's nice to finally meet you."

Rain hammered at the window as Ben shook her hand very gingerly, as if it were covered in spikes.

"This is a carrot-or-stick situation, Mr. Adams. The stick is this: Last week a former Army-Ranger-turned-military-contractor came into the FBI office in LA with a story about a tunnel that rerouted a large portion of the Colorado River underground. He claims to have witnessed you killing three men before being shot in the crotch by you two years ago in Culver City. He also claims that at the same time, your girlfriend killed the CEO of a large agricultural outfit called Agricon. He's having a come-to-Jesus moment and is willing to hang part of it on you by testifying in front of the grand jury. With your history, the bureau is more than happy to go along with another murder prosecution for you, if for no other reason than to make it look like they had it right the first time."

The blood drained out of Ben Adams's face. "Fuck you."

"You know the rules, Mr. Adams. He who breaks the law goes back to the house of pain," she said in a sing-song voice. "At a minimum, I could have you indicted for being a felon in possession of a firearm. Your former-snitch-slash-gun-dealer gave us the story on the .357 you bought from him. I have a go-by for that and could probably knock it together this afternoon and have you indicted by tomorrow morning. The rest we could work out while you sit in the can downtown awaiting trial. I have the search warrant already signed for this shithole apartment right here. Should we start the search? What are the odds that we will find contraband in this apartment? Oh, and as for your girlfriend, we would have to extradite her, but it could be done easily enough; the Kiwis are good that way."

Ben thought of prison. Then he immediately thought of running for it right then and there, but he knew he wouldn't get far. He might make it to Baja with his tent, but he would be penniless. He could fish for food, but sooner or later they would grab him, and that still left Jessica on the hook, assuming they weren't bluffing.

"This all sounds swell. What is the carrot?" he asked, restraining his fury.

"Immunity. For every action related to Agricon. I have the papers right here. All you have to do is cooperate with Special Agent Goodman, stop the shipment, and get the arrest."

Ben looked at Joe with undisguised malice.

"Sorry, man. This is the business, and they knew that you wouldn't do it any other way."

Ben drained his beer and took the papers laid in front of him as the storm raged outside the apartment and in. Ben was good enough at chess to know checkmate when he saw it. They had him dead to rights on the gun charge, and with his background, the jury would probably spend a total of eleven seconds convicting him. That the gun in question had failed him when he needed it most seemed an especially bitter irony at the moment. He quickly signed the paper and threw it down. He walked to his refrigerator and got another heavy stout.

"We're going to leave you with Special Agent Goodman so that you two can get to know each other and go over the case. You are doing the right thing, Ben," Joe said, going to the door with the prosecutor.

Ben didn't say anything; he just exhaled deeply, his arms locked on the countertop, his head hanging down.

After the others had left, Howie came into the kitchen and said, "I'm sorry, boyo, but I really need your help on this, and if it makes you feel any better, I fucking hate the FBI too."

Ben laughed straight at the ground. "Actually, that does make me feel a little better." He straightened. "Beer?"

"Yeah, OK. What the hell?" Howie said, taking the beer as they both went back into the shabby living room to plan. "This isn't a dope deal. We're dealing with a rich businessman here, so this will be way different and hopefully safer than what you're used to."

"Used to? I'm an ex-con. I didn't even work deep cover when I was a fed," Ben explained, still pissed off but trying very hard to see the upside in all of this.

"Right. Sorry. I forgot. This will still be easy. You will go in as yourself, Ben Adams, lawyer and newly minted motorcycle enthusiast. Try not to mention the FBI or ex-con part, but if it comes up, use it to your advantage, and pretend that you are bitter about it."

"Pretend?"

"Even better, channel that," Goodman responded.

"Fine, so what's my in?"

"The guy parties hard, loves adrenaline sports, and is an only child. If you can be his buddy doing the things that he likes to do, it could be enough to get close. We just need to get you to Laguna Seca next week and adjust on the fly. Don't worry; I'm with you all the way on this."

Ben wasn't convinced, but he didn't really have much choice. He knew what jail was like.

21

North Bird Rock, La Jolla, California

After the Homeland Security guy left, Ben finally did paddle out on his Baja board, but he was so distracted that he spent three hours getting a total of two stormy waves. He spent the rest of his time on the ocean fighting the currents and getting hammered by the big sets. When he finally came in, he was destroyed physically and mentally. The rain was still coming down hard as he walked back to his apartment. Geronimo had given up a long time before and was waiting there for him, warm and dry on the patio. Ben hung up his wetsuit and carefully put his board in its place on the rack. He went back into the kitchen and poured himself two fingers of expensive Guatemalan rum, drank it, and poured himself another. His life had gone so far off the rails so many times by this point that he didn't want to dwell too much on his new "job." He tried to distract himself by going to work on Bob's marijuana research. He would need to finish it before starting his new government gig. He knocked it out and produced a quick report detailing the required investment and the proposed regulatory hurdles of opening a legitimate recreational-marijuana shop if the initiative passed. He printed it all out and dropped it on his table to be delivered tomorrow. The wind still rattled the windows as the storm continued its torrent.

Ben felt a distinct psychological fracture build as he drank more rum. Partly, he felt resentment and hostility at being blackmailed, as well as fear of being thrown back in jail, but there was something else; something darker felt like it was waking up. This was the fight-or-flight part of Ben starting to warm up at the thought of another high-stakes life-or-death adventure. Part of Ben wondered if his outrage at the situation was actually manufactured. He might not have wanted to admit this yet, but this might actually be fun. True, this type of fun usually came with bullets, loss of life, and other forms of physical and psychological violence, but as Ben sat back on his torn couch, tumbler of rum in his hand, he smiled, thinking he was about to have a homecoming.

Ben spent the next day trying to prepare for an undercover operation of unnamed parameters and indeterminate length. The threat of prison sat in the back of his brain case like a cinder block. He had signed the deal; why was he still worried?

The storm had lightened up a bit, but the winds and rain were still lashing San Diego. Ben drove his CJ-7 over to Bob's beachfront manse in La Jolla to deliver his research. Geronimo tagged along as always and was well received by the animal doctor.

"That was fast," Bob said upon taking the report and handing Ben a beer.

"I had to rush it. Something came up, and I have to take off in two days."

"Something came up? Knowing your life, that seems unlikely. Family member die?"

"No, the FBI is blackmailing me into helping them on a case," said Ben, lacking the energy to come up with a plausible lie.

"You want to talk about it?" Bob asked with what seemed to Ben like genuine concern.

"Not yet. I am not even sure what I'm into, but thanks, though."

"No sweat, man. Just let me know. Did you paddle out?"

"Yesterday. Not good," Ben said.

"As a medical professional, I should reiterate my advice to steer clear of the ocean until the runoff dissipates. Remember that guy from the cliffs who died of staph?"

"Yeah, yeah," Ben said, waving him off and finishing his beer.

Ben got up to go, and as he walked out the door, he spotted a couple of black Pelican cases sitting in the corner. It had the look of a staging area for some sort of small-scale military operation or maybe a mountaineering expedition.

"What is that?" Ben asked, pointing.

"Nothing, just organizing some of my diving stuff from the garage," Bob responded. Ben thought it looked odd, somehow out of place, but maybe he was just prepping for his own problems and letting it leak into everything else.

22

It took Eric Kaiser only a few days of milking his databases and government contacts in DC to get all the relevant pieces of the Karl Steiger data dump and the subsequent blackmail of Ben Adams. Kaiser had assumed those two idiots had drunk themselves to death by now. He had forgotten all about them and their stories. That they were both talking with the feds added a new wrinkle to his life. He would have to do something about those two. This was his new project.

23

Ben spent his last night of regular citizenship at London's West End. It had no fake kitsch, and from the inside at least, you could have mistaken it for Working Class Milwaukee. The carpet was threadbare, as was the pool table, and it had 1970s-era neon beer signs that had been in place since their birth. Their most recent effort at gentrification was the addition of an Italian panino press, whereby a sandwich would come out from behind the bar and then be grilled in front of the customer. The provenance of the sandwiches was unknown, and thus the panino press sat mostly unused, save for the truly drunk. The upside of London's West End was that the staff didn't mind if Geronimo hung out in there, and the beer was cheap. Ben wandered down around 7:30 p.m., mongrel dog in tow. As he walked in, he saw on the television that ISIS was getting ready to retake Mosul. He flinched and walked over to the bar. He noticed his old "friend" Phil chatting up an attractive blonde at the bar and pulled up a stool next to him, just catching the tail end of a sentence involving "The New World Order and the Chinese gold standard."

"What's up, man?" Ben asked the bleary-eyed Phil.

"Nothin', bro, just telling Daisy here all about the private airline that runs from McCarran Airport out to Area 51."

Ben looked at the girl, then back at Phil.

"Really? Did you tell her about J Rod? Have you heard from him lately?"

Phil ignored the dig about the alien/time traveler known as J Rod, who is said to hang around the cafeteria at Area 51, and continued, "It is legit, bro. Look it up. Janet Airlines is a private contractor; they ferry all the employees on a flight back and forth every day. The parent company is called H, J and J and also makes high-tech electronic triggering devices used in nukes. They are based in San Francisco."

Once again, Phil's combination of insanity and prescience made Ben feel woozy. He ordered a beer and a shot of tequila and went to work on both. He asked the attractive blonde about herself, rather than going any further down Phil's rabbit hole. Ben made normal human small talk with her, which effectively shut Phil out, but Ben just couldn't take it. He felt bad, but he wasn't up to dealing with the black-helicopter crowd tonight, and this girl was a breath of fresh air in the West End. He learned that her name was Daisy, that she was on vacation from Tucson, and that her girlfriends were meeting her tomorrow at their rented condo on the beach not far from the West End. The mention of Tucson put Ben back on his heels a bit, that being the city where part of his Colorado River adventure with Jessica had taken place, the very same adventure that had got him shot and was haunting him now in the form of his new job. Luckily, the booze was starting to take hold, and he soldiered on. They chatted and drank for a few hours, the three of them doing many tequila shots. Eventually, Phil got tired of being ignored and wandered over to the pool table. There was no loss. Had Ben not come along, Phil would have gone on about Area 51. She surely would have bolted. Not to mention, dogs are irresistible. Daisy played with Geronimo under the bar in between drinks, and they laughed and flirted almost like normal people.

Back at Ben's apartment, they fell almost instantly into bed, Daisy straddling him as he fell on his back. They undressed each other urgently. He started to sit up, and she pushed him backward and slid on top of him. Ben watched her rhythmically move her head back, relishing every moment. Ben closed his eyes to do the same. He felt her hand go to his nose forcefully as he inhaled, and before he could question it, his nervous system flooded with feel-good chemicals.

Cocaine? Really?

Daisy giggled as she pulled her hand away and gave herself a bump. The Peruvian stimulant flooded Ben's bloodstream. He decided to let go. His last memory of that night was Daisy's face grinning down at him from above in chemical and physical pleasure.

The next morning, Ben awoke already recognizing the early onset of a building shame spiral. The indictment of daylight played through his blinds as he picked his way through the runaway party detritus. He blearily looked around the apartment and garage. No Daisy and no Geronimo. He was pretty sure Geronimo couldn't be stolen.

Maybe he went willingly. Ben thought back on their years together, then looked around his apartment and had to concede that if the dog had taken off with Daisy, he wouldn't hold it against him.

He sat back on the couch and closed his eyes.

"So who is Jessica?" Daisy asked, holding his phone.

Ben snapped out of his torpor and looked at last night's assailant/lover. She stood in the doorway with Geronimo and two giant coffees from the cart by the pier and what looked like a bag of donuts.

"She looks cute," she finished, tossing the phone to Ben.

He looked at his phone, and there was a picture of Jessica in a bikini top and shorts, looking fantastic in front of their old beach shack in Raglan, with the text "You should come back."

"Where does she want you to go?" Daisy asked in a mock pout.

"New Zealand," Ben responded robotically.

"Really?"

Ben arched his eyebrows and glanced at her.

"Wow, no offense, but why aren't you on a plane right now?"

Ben didn't have an answer. They made superficial and awkward small talk, and after about thirty minutes, Daisy left. She left the door open. Geronimo watched but didn't follow her out.

24

en got his jeep ready in a way that was becoming
a little too familiar, planning for a trip of unknown duration and destination, and flicked
on the fluorescent lights of his operating room–clean
garage. He packed his newly acquired pistol, the third
of his illegally obtained firearms, in the center console
of the jeep. The first didn't work, and the second was
stolen by a cartel *sicario*, so hopefully the third time
was the charm. This trip would test his nerve as well
as his meager acting skills. The pistol might come in
handy. The weather was still terrible, so Ben put on the
vinyl soft-top, Geronimo jumped into the old CJ, and
they rolled north.

Ben had his instructions to participate in the motorcycle class, make contact with Mr. Trentino, and
then meet with Special Agent Goodman in his hotel
room. That didn't give him much to go on, but maybe

that was better. He felt pretty hemmed in already, and any micromanagement had the potential to push him over the edge.

With the exception of Camp Pendleton, from Tijuana to Malibu, Southern California was completely paved over. Ben took PCH through Redondo and Manhattan Beach to avoid a crash on the 405 and drove through the "town" of El Segundo, cleverly named by Standard Oil as their second large oil refinery on the West Coast. Out of habit, Ben looked for Pratte's Reef, a multimillion-dollar joke of a thing paid for by Chevron as part of a settlement for their destruction of that part of the coast. Made out of sandbags to replace the surfable waves that Chevron had destroyed and for fish habitat, it had never lived up to either promise. In fact, it was hard to even spot it. Man still hadn't figured out how to improve on what the earth had perfected.

It took a few hours to escape the Tijuana/San Diego/Los Angeles megacity, but they ultimately hooked it left back onto PCH and north through Malibu along the coast. The farther they drove, the more it felt like going backward in time. The farms and vineyards of Ventura County replaced the urban sprawl of Southern California; it could have been fifty years ago. Ben rubbernecked a surf spot called Rincon, otherwise known as "the Queen of the Coast," as he passed, catching a glimpse of one of the finest point breaks in the world ripping along the shore, some lucky soul carried with it on his longboard. Turning inland, they continued on Highway 1. They ran parallel to the fabled Hollister Ranch, a cautionary tale for surf paradise lost as powerful as anything Milton could write and as true as can be. They couldn't see it any longer, but they knew it was there. It is now locked up and available to only the richest of the rich. The Hollister name now a punch line to the surfing community, a hollow sound for tweens to buy into at malls in the inland deserts. Ben had never surfed The Ranch. Few had, but the satellite imagery of the Internet had allowed him to stare at its coast for many years.

The rhythm of the road lulled him into complacency. He had all day to make the trip, and he had started early, so they stopped for a lunch of fried seafood and clam chowder in Morro Bay and watched the birds dive at the ocean. They kept heading north. With every mile north, the ocean grew sharkier. It didn't seem to stop plenty of people from surfing, even within the Red Triangle. Ben figured he would probably have done the same if he lived there, the great whites just another risk factor in a totally messed up world. Continuing north, Ben tried not to notice the late-model Chevy sedan that stayed about five cars back at all times. He assumed it was Special Agent Goodman keeping tabs on him. They passed San Simeon while Ben tossed around an unformed idea about the powerful and the powerless and where he was on that spectrum as compared to Randolph Hearst in his day. He let that thought blow out the window as it threatened to take over his drive. It was a nice day, and tomorrow was fucked. Best to just enjoy the ride.

Max speed on the jeep was about seventy-five, and Ben kept it at around seventy so as not to stress it. Donovan's "Season of the Witch" bubbled out of his dashboard speakers, barely audible over the wind. A group of bikers blew by him at eighty-five-plus, their straight pipes rattling the windshield. From Ben's days as a fed, he recognized the patches on their vests as belonging to one of the many California outlaw biker gangs the FBI and ATF were always running ops against for drugs and guns. The last guy in the pack was riding a stripped-down hardtail with a springer front end, 1920s technology designed for maybe thirty-five miles per hour. He had a gray ponytail blowing out from under his barely legal helmet. The shape of which was presumably intended to evoke World War II–era Nazi storm troopers. To Ben it just made the guy look like a penis, coronal ridge and all. He smirked at this thought as he watched the biker blast by him.

After he got a few bike lengths ahead, Ben noticed the rear of the chopper start to sway, oscillating wider and wider until the rear tire exploded in a cloud of white smoke and strips of rubber. The bike went sideways, and the dickhead went flying. Ben swerved to avoid the wreck and the tumbling body as some of the other bikers peeled off to help. Some conspicuously kept on, ignoring the crash and their fallen comrade. Ben guessed correctly that they wouldn't stand up to any law-enforcement scrutiny and thus left their friend to fend for himself. At this point, Ben couldn't be particularly judgmental. In another life, he might have stopped to help, but he had his own issues at the moment, so he stayed on task. In a sense, he had become like the bikers, an outlaw lurching from one savage instinct to the next while trying to stay out of a cage. One last glance in the rearview and he kept driving.

As they kept going north toward Monterey through the coastal grasslands, Ben thought about Steinbeck. Ben had just finished reading *Tortilla Flat* and chuckled to himself at the Arthurian legend interpreted through some wine-addled *paesanos*. He definitely saw some parallels from his life reflected back in that book. He and his "friends" at the beach weren't too far off from the self-deluded and often self-destructive lives of the characters of *Tortilla Flat*. He could relate to their perennial search for wine and oblivion. Certainly he drank as much as they did.

25

Central California Coast

Ben and Geronimo pulled into the parking lot of their hotel in Carmel-by-the-Sea.

As opposed to Carmel-by-the-Freeway?

They parked next to a red Ferrari, and on the other side was a Chevy Monte Carlo with the telltale window tint and antenna of a government car. Goodman was already here. This was not the car that had followed him today; somebody else was watching. Ben and Geronimo walked into the lobby to check in. Say what you will about California snobbery, but they are incredibly tolerant of dogs, which Ben thought speaks much for them as a group. It was a small hotel built in the '50s or '60s that had been remodeled at great expense into a "boutique" hotel, whatever the hell that meant. It was a decent place to lay your head, at any rate. Ben dumped his stuff and left G-dog in the room with a promise of leftovers and made his way down to the bar. There had been several high-dollar BMW motorcycles in the parking lot, and he therefore assumed that some of his schoolmates were staying in the same hotel. He wandered into the bar and grabbed a stool. The bartender, a charming and attractive red-haired girl, took his order for a local brew and dropped a menu. Ben glanced over his shoulder at the crowd in the bar/dining room. A gathering of about ten mixed-age people was celebrating a birthday or anniversary or something, and there was a DJ setting up in front of their tables. A group of four guys in their early forties wearing riding leathers was arguing loudly over some motorcycle-related minutiae, which ultimately devolved into ululating at the one Middle Eastern–looking guy in the group. Ben saw Giancarlo Trentino on the other side of the room sitting at a low two-top, eating a salad, and drinking either a double vodka tonic or a sparkling water with lime. He wasn't alone. The girl with him was, to undersell it, startling in her beauty. Five foot ten, in spectacular shape, with long, wavy black hair and a vaguely Mediterranean look to her, she nibbled on something green and nursed what Ben guessed was a cosmopolitan. She appeared to be pouting, but Trentino didn't seem to be biting. They ate in silence, periodically checking their phones. Ben couldn't be sure, but the way Giancarlo was looking at the table of middle-aged motorcycle hooligans, there might have been something to SA Goodman's theory that maybe he needed a pal. With the girl at the table, Ben wasn't going to be able to make a move here. He turned his attention to the table of motorcyclists, which had reached max volume, including a full mooning from one to the other three followed by some moderate ass slapping. Ben ordered a Cubano sandwich, hoping for the best in a place that had to be five thousand miles from Cuba. He kept his eye on his target using the mirror behind the bar. A text appeared on his phone from a blocked number that simply read, "Room 504." *Goodman.*

Ben finished his sandwich and headed upstairs to meet with his new handler. As he left he saw Trentino and his date getting ready to leave and the table full of rowdy riders ordering a round of shots. He arrived at room 504 and knocked.

"Who is it?" came the voice of the case agent.

"The tooth fairy. Who do you think?" answered Ben.

The door swung open, and Ben stepped inside as Howard peered into the hallway to make sure nobody had seen Ben come in.

"So how did it go?" Goodman asked.

"How did what go? I just got here."

"I know, I know. I just wanted to know if you had anything yet," he said a bit nervously.

"Jesus Christ, Is this your first case?" Ben asked, now more leery than before.

"God, no, but this is one of the biggest and riskiest for various reasons, not the least of which is that our undercover operative is straight from the fringe of society. No offense."

"Fair point. I saw your guy and his Amazon girlfriend in the lobby. They seemed pretty serious. It didn't look like I could make an advance, but I'll take a shot tomorrow at the track."

"Good, good. Don't push it. We want to get this done, but we don't want to blow it. We have a little time. Take little bites. Your only goal for the moment is to become his friend and see if he drops something, and we will go from there and hook up again tomorrow night and debrief."

"Hey, who else is on this case? I saw another G-ride following me today."

"Nobody else, man. Just you and me. You sure they were following you?"

"Not entirely sure. Maybe it was a coincidence," Ben said, not believing a word he had just said. "Am I dismissed?" he was tired from the long drive and from having someone to report to.

"Totally. Get some rest, get to the track early, and try and have some fun with this. I know part of you misses the job."

"Don't count on it," Ben said, leaving the room and making his way back down to the bar, having forgotten to get Geronimo a snack. The guys in the leathers were still hammering back drinks as Ben made his way back to his room with a steak sandwich for a very grateful dog.

26

Early the next morning, Ben and Geronimo worked their way down to the parking lot, stopping first for coffee and a bagel in the lobby. Say what you will about so-called boutique hotels; the coffee was freaking good, and the bagel had East Coast written all over it. Ben looked down at the map in his hands with printed directions to Laguna Seca Raceway; he had been assured by his masters at Homeland Security that he had a slot in the class. The track was built in the 1950s out of the remnants of the old Laguna Seca Ranch, a pretty seaside location close to absurd amounts of wealth. It is famous for the Corkscrew, otherwise known as turn eight. It is photogenic and terrifying to take at speed. Anyone who has seen road racing on television or a magazine ad for high-dollar watches has seen it. The Corkscrew is actually a combination of two turns: a hard left immediately followed by a hard right. It starts as a blind uphill then drops forty feet downhill, banking right. For fans of physics, it means that whatever vehicle you are in or on, be it car or motorcycle, the turn compresses the suspension, and it loads up on the uphill and then re-leases it on the downhill, taking the weight of the ve-hicle off the tires all while trying to effect back-to-back ninety-degree turns. It makes for spectacular photos and videos, and the tales of horror among riders and drivers are legion.

Ben pondered all this as he drove through the hilly grasslands of California's Central Coast en route to the track. He forgot his mission for a moment and was just cruising with his dog, catching the warm sun and sea breeze through the unzipped windows of the jeep. He rolled up to the track facility and attempted to navigate the maze of roads and driveways that would normally direct spectators, race cars, and tractor trail-ers to their appropriate places, but today the track was quiet, strictly a private event. He finally figured out where he needed to be and drove his jeep into the pit area. He saw the same Ferrari and BMW motorcycles from last night as well as several other high-dollar vehi-cles: one Tesla, a Pagani Zonda, and an Aston Martin Vanquish. This group clearly liked to go fast. Ben, the dog, and the CJ-7 did not fit in.

Historically, Ben's enthusiasm for motorcycles was moderate at best; however, when he walked through the pits past the row of new BMW S1000RRs, he had to admit that there was some sort of primal appeal there. These were the bikes they would be riding for the class, $20,000 each, 180 horsepower of two-wheeled organ-donation machines.

Ben's mind jangled as he thought about what he was about to do. This was his first deep-cover assignment ever. He wasn't even an FBI agent anymore, and whatever light undercover work he had done, it was a long, long time ago. Further, he was entering a world of which he knew virtually nothing.

Motorcycle racing?

Ben tried to relax a bit when he realized he didn't really give a fuck, but then he oscillated right back to anxiety when he remembered that if this didn't go well, there was a prison cell with his name on it. He had done five years that way; he would not go back.

He checked in at the catering table with the pretty blonde there. She looked him up and down, which flattered Ben a bit, until he realized that it was likely part of her job description. He joined the other riders in an empty garage filled with several dozen chairs and set up with a portable movie screen. The boisterous gang from last night was already there, along with a handful of young, serious-looking, very fit racer types, including one short, tattooed female rider in ripped physical condition sporting a pink Mohawk. There were several older, paunchier weekend-warrior/midlife-crisis types milling about as well. It was quickly clear to Ben that this was just another subculture like surfing or any sport, with its own jargon, slang, hierarchy, and mythology. He kept catching references to Valentino Rossi, of whom Ben knew nothing except that he is nicknamed "The Doctor" and was somehow important to this group. It reminded him of the floor in the FBI building that housed the Joint Terrorism Task Force. If you lingered too long up there getting coffee, you would experience what could best be described as a game of "Celebrity Terrorist Name Dropping." For example, if someone dropped an "Al Zarqawi," then someone else would have to see that and raise them with a story involving "Abu Zubaydah." If they really wanted to land it, they would let it be known that they had got their information from the CIA SCIF in the building, preferably that day. They were like a troop of chimps establishing the social hierarchy, but with suits, guns, and coffee. He dismissed those memories as both irrelevant and unpleasant and returned his attention to the group.

Giancarlo was in the front row and looking ready to go. Ben looked up at the diagram of Laguna Seca at the front of the room and recalled his high-speed vehicular-pursuit training at the FBI academy. They had done a fair amount of driving there in old Impalas and Crown Vics, and although it wasn't on a motor-cycle, Ben thought that maybe some of the same principles would apply. This gave him comfort in knowing that he had at least one intellectual handhold on this situation, one that maybe he could build on and avoid killing himself at one hundred miles per hour.

The instructor gave a briefing and history of the track and a description of the bikes they would be riding. Everyone introduced themselves, including their motorcycle riding/racing résumés. The instructor then discussed the format. There would be riding sessions mixed with academic sessions. This would give the riders a chance to learn something new and rest at the same time. The good news for Ben was that the riders, regardless of ability, would all be on the track at the same time. If he was going to befriend this guy, it would have to be over a shared experience. When the time came for the first classroom session, Ben noticed the stratification: he was in the rookie section, the drunks from the night before were in the intermediate group, and Giancarlo and the other lean-looking guys were clearly in the pro group. It didn't matter: as soon as class time was over, they were all hitting the track. Ben sat down with a very punk-looking instructor named Dan who was an aspiring road racer himself and taught these courses as a way to cover the bills until he either made it big or killed himself. Dan went over the basics of riding around a track. It was all very familiar to Ben from his FBI training in terms of where to enter a turn, what an apex was, how to hit it, whether it was early or late, decreasing and increasing radius turns. Ben started feeling a bit more confident.

27

It was time to ride. Ben had been given a loaner set of gear, which included a helmet, leathers, and boots and gloves, all Kevlar reinforced and all with telltale crash damage from previous users. It was not encouraging. Geronimo wasn't into it and left to hang out with the pretty blonde in the shade by the lunch table. The entire group got on their bikes and fired them up. The instructors let loose with a grave admonition that the tires on the motorcycles were cold and to hold back for the first lap until they got sticky. Ben hadn't thought of that.

Cold tires?

Ben hit the starter, and the big BMW roared to life. He teased the throttle a little bit and felt the shudder and vibration beneath him. He noticed that the instruments did not include a speedometer. He looked around and realized that with the helmets on, he would not be able to identify the individual riders by their faces but by their gear. Most of the rookies had the same crappy loaner gear that Ben had, but the others had custom, presumably high-dollar leathers that would make them easier to spot. Giancarlo was in all black. The LA guys were all wearing outrageous fluorescent colors to match their attitudes. He took this all in as they awaited the green flag. At this point Ben's instructions from Dan had been simple: just ride the track, and don't crash.

The green flag dropped, and the LA whackos roared off, cold tires and all. The pros followed cautiously, knowing the penalty for failure. Ben and his crew rolled onto the track last, Ben starting to sweat as he began to grasp the potential for speed and death. He put his true purpose here out of his mind and tried to stay focused on the task at hand, namely getting around the track with the rubber side of the motorcycle down. The group entered the track from the pits right after turn two. Ben was just getting on the throttle as he saw the first group entering turn three, a medium-speed right-hander. He quickly grasped the cold-tire issue as he saw one of the LA roosters lose the back end of his bike and start to slide sideways, managing to catch it at the last second and stay upright. There was a chorus of motorcycle horns as comment from his friends. Several of the instructors shook their helmets. They knew the type; they were the type. The group started building their speed. Ben guessed they were doing maybe sixty miles per hour on the straight sections and twenty to forty in the turns, which didn't seem too bad. Maybe he could do this.

They blasted uphill, approaching the dreaded Corkscrew, and when they hit it, Ben immediately understood its menace. Blind on the approach and followed by a huge drop, it took a literal leap of faith that your bike was pointed for the exit, because you couldn't see a thing. The remaining few turns were easy in comparison. They made the last hard left at turn eleven and hit the straight. Tires warm, everyone took off like bullets. Ben hit the throttle and followed without thinking about it. The first lap was a joke. Now his front wheel came off the ground, touching only between gears. He very nearly slid off the back of the bike; he had to grip with his entire body to stay on. They ripped down the straight toward turn one, which on the map looked like just a slight bend in the track, but at this speed turn one looked like a hard ninety degrees. It was fucking terrifying. Ben was in sixth gear at full throttle. He had no idea how fast he was going, but the grandstands were a blur. He lost his nerve and hit the brakes as he watched the better riders take it at speed and start to shrink from him into the distance.

Morning lessons included instruction on how to keep the bike/rider center of gravity as low as possible in the turns while keeping the bike as upright as possible. The reason being that the best traction for a motorcycle is dead upright. The more it is leaned over, the more likely it is that the tires will slide. In practice, this meant getting as close to the ground with your body while still remaining on the bike. Ben had learned this and was having trouble with it. The idea was to change the geometry and center of gravity with your body, meaning getting your head as close to the pavement as possible at extraordinary speed. He zoomed around the track with the group, but the other racers were lapping him as if he didn't exist. More than once, he saw the blur of his target, Giancarlo, flash past him at high speed through a turn. The LA crew was passing him as well, not quite as fast as the pros but much more recklessly. He had enough natural talent to stay in front of the other rookies, though, and even lapped one or two of the more inept ones. But with each lap he grew faster; with each turn, his face got closer to the ground, the red-and-white track striping flickering a strobe in his now narrowed peripheral vision. Just as he was entering a flow state, the white flag went out, indicating their last lap for that session. He gave it everything he had and knew his speed had improved. Giancarlo ripped past him in turn six, and Ben kept up with him long enough to notice that he slowed way down for the Corkscrew, as did everyone else. Ben sensed an opening.

Everyone pulled off for the next lecture. The group was starting to warm up to one another a bit, engaging in some light banter about the session. The LA crew was taking the piss out of one another. Each one claiming that the others sucked and that any lack of victory in any given scenario was the result of unforeseen and unavoidable forces and had absolutely nothing to do with their immutable riding prowess. Ben laughed to himself at their antics while he tracked down his dog. He then went over to one of the garages for more intel on how to ride that horrifying bike. As he was walking, he noticed another rider he hadn't seen before. He was an Asian man in his forties, not tall, but he walked like a coiled spring. He had older, expensive black leathers and a matching black helmet; neither of them had a mark on them. This man clearly did not crash. At the risk of insensitive cultural stereotyping, Ben thought the guy looked like a ninja. They made eye contact as they passed in opposite directions and held each other's gaze for longer than was comfortable. To anyone else in the garage, it would have looked like those two were either in love or were about to kill each other. Ben tightened up, ready for something, but the ninja kept walking.

After about thirty minutes of lecture by Dan, Ben's takeaway from the lesson was to use his core strength to hold himself on the bike, keeping his arms loose to make small inputs into the handlebars. It was not unlike the grip required to fire a gun accurately, letting his body do the work so he could just squeeze the trigger. Up to that point, Ben had been white-knuckling it around the track.

Ben took this information to heart and thought about applying it as he got up and left the garage. As he walked out into the sunlight and toward the motorcycles, he noticed a figure in the grandstands with a pair of binoculars.

Real subtle, Goodman.

He scanned the horizon and then noticed another figure with binoculars standing on a hillside above turn six.

Maybe that is Goodman?

This track probably attracted a lot of lookie-loos, but something about the stance of the figure suggested a more pointed intention. This didn't bode well. Ben ignored it as irrelevant for the moment as he tried to focus on the bike.

The group sprinted out to their bikes to begin the next track session; they were positively aching for another adrenal spike. Ben was going to use his new knowledge to try to keep up with Giancarlo and possibly overtake him. He hoped he could find his opening out there. When the green flag dropped, he made sure to take off with the LA group. Ben had many faults, but he was a good student, and he was applying his new skills well. He found that he could now keep up with the LA group and even beat some of them through certain sections. He also noticed that as fatigue set in, their courage and competitiveness started to dramatically exceed their skills. They were on the ragged edge of crashing the entire time. Ben was hanging at the back of their pack, waiting for his opportunity to move on his target, when they rounded turn eleven going into the straight. All the riders hammered their throttles and blasted off, every one of their front wheels just barely airborne. It was now a game of chicken. They all roared down the straight, but Ben had finally had enough and backed off the throttle at midway through sixth gear. The others stayed on, not wanting to be the first person to cave. Three of the group finally capitulated and braked, but for the guy in front, it was too late: he would never make the turn. He didn't even try to touch the brakes as he straightlined it off the track in a cloud of dust and a yard sale of machinery and rider. The other three made the turn, going slowly enough to raise their middle fingers and blast their horns at the rider on the ground, the guy picking himself up and walking over to the downed motorcycle.

Coming out of turn two, Ben saw Giancarlo trying to make his move in his peripheral vision. Giancarlo was clearly the better rider, but Ben was getting harder to pass. Coming onto the straight out of turn four, Trentino made his move. This was the opportunity Ben was hoping for. The Corkscrew was so scary that most riders held way back just to get through it, and were usually too scared to make a pass there. This meant Ben could leverage everyone else's fear and try to make his move there. The other good news was that because of the tightness of the turns and the elevator drop out of the back, it was pretty much the slowest part of the track. He thought it just might work, and if it went bad, at least he would be going relatively slowly when he crashed. He just had to stay on his tires and stay with Giancarlo for three more turns.

He locked on to the better rider's rear tire and would not let go through turns five, six, and seven. He was definitely back into white-knuckle territory. He was almost horizontal going through turn six, his knee dragging loudly on the pavement and his face looking at his front brakes. At least he wouldn't have far to fall if he lost it. He straightened up coming out of six and banked right into seven. Giancarlo got onto the brakes hard to go left into the Corkscrew, and Ben held off for just a second and rolled up right next to him on the inside. He finally hammered his brakes hard, and both bikes leaned left, their riders' knees on the ground. Ben could feel Trentino over his right shoulder. His back tire started to slide as he made the transition to the right-hand turn, and the bottom dropped out. He was momentarily airborne. He landed and ripped open the throttle as he slid sideways. He had done it. He pulled himself together and blasted into turn nine, going too fast to look over his shoulder and see what had happened to Trentino.

Maybe he crashed?

A blur in black leathers angrily flashed past within inches and was gone. On the next turn, he saw the white flag signaling the last lap before lunch. Ben lowered his intensity level to about 75 percent for the last lap as he brought his heart rate down. He had made his move; he could apologize to Trentino and hopefully gain some measure of friendship and take it from there. As he cruised his last lap, he saw the LA guy walking his now destroyed motorcycle back toward the pits from the straight where he had crashed, seemingly without major injury.

Everybody still upright parked their bikes and dismounted. Ben pulled off his helmet and started over to where Trentino had just pulled in. He walked toward him with palms upright and a large smile indicating sorrow and supplication. He hoped this would ingratiate him and create some sort of exploitable relationship. Trentino made eye contact, jumped off his bike, ripped off his helmet, and charged at Ben, fury in his eyes. Geronimo saw the threat and bolted from the sanctity of the snack table toward the fray, but Giancarlo got to Ben first.

"What the fuck is wrong with you?" he screamed as he approached Ben and wound up for a haymaker.

He let fly with the wild punch, but this was not Ben's first rodeo, and he dodged it easily, grabbing Trentino's wrist and pinning it to his own hip while he drove his forearm into Trentino's triceps, making an arm bar and taking him surgically to the ground. This was not what Ben had expected, but he improvised. On the ground, his face in the pavement, Trentino struggled. Ben leaned in close to his ear and, in a moment of inspired improvisation, growled quietly, "How do you ever expect to win a race riding like such a pussy?"

Giancarlo stopped struggling, his face slack for a moment. After a beat, he broke into a huge grin and started laughing into the pavement, dust swirling around his face. Recognizing the threat as having passed, Geronimo sat down to watch.

"I have no fucking idea," he said, still laughing. Ben slowly released him, and they both got to their feet. Giancarlo offered his hand, and Ben took it. "That was still a fucked-up move, you know?"

"I'll buy you a Coke and some chips from Julie at the snack table," said Ben, admitting no wrong.

"Fair enough." Trentino clapped him on the shoulder as they walked over to the shade.

By then the LA gang had caught up to them and started reliving the moment, with Ben clearly the hero for the time being, based entirely on his recklessness. They seemed to appreciate a near total disregard for human life. They all walked to a catered lunch, back-slapping and laughing as the adrenaline faded from their bloodstreams.

As they sat around a large table and made small talk, Ben worked his lawyer-from-San-Diego story and got to know everybody. The group from LA were all college buddies who had made it good in finance and got together a few times a year to pretend they were still young and scare the shit out of themselves. Giancarlo also warmed up and seemed to be having a good time.

He gave a straightforward version of his professional life, his father, and his business. Ben noticed that he left off the part about selling high-tech munitions to the Middle East in violation of several very toothy federal laws. But as the group chatted and ate in genuine bonhomie, Ben felt the roots of the undercover op start to form. He also started to feel the telltale UC conflict brewing, namely that he was building a relationship with someone he was ultimately going to destroy. They relived their most terrifying moments on the track and laughed at all their moments of failure. The two most celebrated were the NASA-style launch into the dirt at the end of the straight and Ben's airborne Corkscrew pass of Giancarlo.

28

Ben actually liked these guys, and in another life he felt like he could have been one of them. They had the same adrenal deficiency as Ben, but instead of treating it with intrigue, gunfights, and murder, they just took it to the racetrack in an altogether less violent outlet. Although, after what Ben had witnessed that day, he thought he might actually outlive these clowns.

As they geared up for the last session of the day, the head instructor came out and asked how everybody was doing and if there were any questions. With the exception of the pros, almost everybody was spent, that level of physical effort and mental focus having taken a toll on the middle-aged Walter Mittys. Finally, the instructor asked by a show of hands if anyone was uncomfortable with the level of aggression and/or passing distances. At a shot, all four hands from the LA guys went up.

"Nope, nope, you assholes don't count," the instructor said, waving them down. "Anybody else?"

The instructor concluded and told them to get to the start/finish line in five minutes. In what was possibly a moment of weakness, Giancarlo invited everyone at the table to Monte Carlo in two weeks for the Formula One race. He had expensed a suite overlooking the track, and all were welcome. A series of high fives went around as everyone greedily accepted, including Ben. He wasn't sure how well his acting skills were holding up, but he was making progress in the right direction. Monte Carlo. That had to be where the deal was going to go down.

There was a new bike for the nutcase who had crashed, and the rest of the day passed without serious incident. Ben traded paint with a guy in turn five, but it was accidental, and everyone stayed upright. By the time the checkered flag dropped, everyone was glad it was over. They looked beat. They retreated to the hotel bar, dog included. Giancarlo bought the first round, and everybody roared approval. Ben was pleased to start drinking again. It was his happy place. They kept on about the track and the turns, comparing lap times and making excuses why they weren't in first place on every single lap. After about half an hour, Giancarlo's girlfriend came in. She grabbed a white wine and acted put out by the revelry of such a sweaty and disgusting group of drunks. Ben was enjoying himself, happy to feel the booze and actually forget for the moment why he was here. She brought him back to reality, and not in a good way.

Giancarlo introduced her as Sophia, and she nodded curtly to the assembled mob. In any normal setting, all eyes would have been riveted on her, but these guys were just too wasted in every sense. Ben kept looking at her out of the corner of his eye as he tried to make bawdy jokes and fit in. Something was just not quite right. Her pouty gold-digger routine didn't quite fit. She had a certain tension. He could see it in the striated muscles she was flaunting in her off-the-shoulder dress. She had an incredible body but almost on the wrong side of feminine. Ben felt like he recognized someone who was playing a part. *Maybe that is how girls act toward guys with money.* Ben couldn't pin it down. Giancarlo reiterated his Monte Carlo invite, which prompted another round of cheers, jeers, and drinks. After about an hour, the group started to settle down a bit. Ben deliberately chatted up Giancarlo.

"What have you got going the next two weeks before Monte Carlo?" Ben asked.

"Sophia and I are going to climb the Nose Route on El Capitan in Yosemite," he replied in a manner far too casual to contain the reality of that statement.

Ben didn't climb mountains, but he knew enough to know that this was a serious climbing objective. He had absolutely no interest in anything like it but felt like he should push it for the sake of staying out of jail.

"You looking for another climber?" Ben asked.

"How much climbing have you done?" Giancarlo asked skeptically.

"Not much," Ben said, hugely exaggerating his experience and sending a handful of french fries under the bar for Geronimo. Giancarlo squinted at the undercover man.

"I think maybe not, man. The Nose of El Cap is strictly 'experts only.' You know what I mean? Plus, climbing with three is a little weird. Let's catch up in Monte Carlo. I'll text you all the details. If you haven't been, you will dig it!" he said, taking Sophia by the hand and leaving the bar.

29

Ben wasn't super excited about briefing Goodman, so he drained another straight Jameson's before he bade everyone farewell and made his way upstairs, Geronimo trotting happily behind. He knocked on the door, and a rather harried Special Agent Goodman let them in.

"It took you long enough. What did you get?" he asked urgently.

"It looks like it's going down in Monte Carlo in two weeks. You…are…welcome," said Ben, slightly slurring his words.

"How do you know?"

"Because that's where he's going, and it's a perfect transshipment point to the Middle East," said Ben, surprising himself at remembering some of the vernacular of the investigation. He also mentioned the climbing trip.

"He told you this?" said Goodman, scribbling it all down.

"Yep. He invited all of us to his suite to watch the Formula One race. It's a perfect cover to do a deal. So…good luck with all that," said Ben, waving his hand in a circle, eyes half-closed.

"Cool, so that gives us enough time to prep the op and get you ready for your trip."

"Negative, dude. You got your intel, and I am off of the hook," said Ben, eyes now fully closed.

"How do you know? He's going to Europe. You're probably right, but we won't know until you get there and confirm. You are in. You've done a good job so far. Don't fuck us over now."

"Howie, I don't even have a passport anymore," Ben croaked, feeling the noose tightening.

"Bullshit, *dude.* I checked with State right before we got started. You renewed eighteen months ago. You are good for eight and a half more years. Go ahead and tell me you lost it, and I will expedite a new one— be in San Diego in two days. This is going to happen. Don't go sideways on me now. I know a guy at the Park Service, I will have him make sure the climbing trip is legit and have him keep eyes on them while we get you prepped for Europe."

Ben knew he was beat, and he was drunk enough to let it ride. At least he didn't have to climb El Capitan. He ripped off a big raspberry toward the earnest special agent, lumbered to his feet, and started for the door. He silently motioned for Geronimo to join him, and the dog jumped up and started out as well. Ben spotted a bottle of vodka on the table and grabbed it on his way out. Special Agent Goodman waved him on, shaking his head.

30

Ben woke the next day with his head pounding in what was becoming a routine ailment. He packed his bags and walked down to the lobby. It was a small comfort that the LA crew was there and looked pretty torn up as well. They were decked out in their riding gear for the long trip down the coast. The jeep did not have much in the way of comfort, but he did not envy the day those guys had in front of them. They checked out and made small talk in the bar, which, while seeming like returning to the scene of a crime, served only coffee and pastries at this hour. Ben told them that it looked like he would be seeing them in Monte Carlo after all. Sheepish looks and excuses followed from the group. It seemed that in their exuberance the night before, they had forgotten that they had careers and families to contend with and that a last-minute boys' trip to Monte Carlo might not fly with the bosses and wives. There was apparently a rather large and important youth soccer tournament that if missed would generate large legal fees for the divorce attorneys. Ben was on his own and genuinely disappointed. Maybe he, like Giancarlo, needed some buddies as well. His mind hardened a bit at that thought, and he realized that for the job at hand, a bunch of extraneous drunken civilians might be bad for the operation. They migrated out to the parking lot to go their separate ways. Ben noticed that the Ferrari was gone. Trentino and his partner must have checked out early to get to Yosemite. Ben hoped to hell that this deal would get done there, that the Park Service would make the arrest, and that he would be off the hook, but he knew it was never that easy.

Ben drove all day back to San Diego, reversing his trip from a few days before. By all accounts, he had been successful. He even received an attaboy via text from his old friend Joe Lanahan. Cloud cover socked in the coast, mirroring Ben's mood as he motored down Pacific Coast Highway. Geronimo didn't care at all. He hung his head out of the jeep, tongue lolling out. His day couldn't be better. Ben could feel the stirrings of his old self trying to do some good in the world. A noble cause and the adrenaline of high-stakes law enforcement were appealing on some level, but he had been screwed over so many times that the urge to be left the fuck alone so he could surf almost eclipsed all other emotions. He went in circles like this for the entire drive to San Diego, each time realizing he was cornered. The internal debate was not only in-dicative of dicey mental health but also absolutely useless. He noticed the Ford sedan trailing him the entire time and hoped it was Homeland Security keeping an eye on their asset.

Back at his apartment, he prepped for his trip. Normally, this would have involved assembling out-door gear and making sure his rig was mechanically sound and his weaponry was in good working order. Things were different this time. He was way off the map, going undercover to Europe. He realized that to pull off this charade, he was going to need an upgrade to his wardrobe. Even Ben wasn't so detached that he didn't know Monte Carlo would require something at least slightly more legit than the San Diego–spec board shorts, T-shirt, and flip-flops. So he went shop-ping. He hadn't done anything like this since his FBI days, where coat and tie were required office wear. In fact, he was as fit as he had ever been, and his old FBI wardrobe would have been fine had he not burned it all in a giant bonfire in Baja after he was released from prison. Not knowing any better about current fashion, Ben broke out his American Express Platinum Card and went to the nicest men's store he could find in La Jolla. By the time he left, he could have passed for wealthy and powerful in any enclave in the world. It was terrible.

Back at the house, he packed all his new clothes into a waterproof duffel bag designed for wetsuits, feeling like he was going to a costume party. He shoved that thought back down and kept packing. As screwed up as he was from losing his career and spending five years in Pelican Bay, in the end he had won: he had his freedom, and he had money. It was all in jeopardy now if he didn't do everything right. That his victory had been entirely pyrrhic was lost on him in his alcohol- and PTSD-addled mind. He walked to his fortress of a garage, opened the door, and turned on the lights. The bright fluorescents flooded the spotless space with clean, bright light. He walked past his rack of surfboards and wetsuits without a second glance and straight to his tool chest. He pulled out a small head-lamp; a tactical flashlight; and a lightweight, folding Spyderco knife. Ben might have been stupid enough to take this assignment, but he wasn't going naked.

He then walked over to a closet and grabbed some tan, milspec BDU pants, a handful of black cotton polo shirts, and a pair of Nike Field boots that looked a lot like standard-issue Vietnam War–era jungle boots, but with the latest in materials and technology. If he had put the outfit together, Ben would have looked like a firearms instructor from South Carolina, but if he had needed to run or fight and still not look like a psycho, it would have worked. It was a strange thing to do, but somehow it gave him comfort. His bag packed, he only needed to sort out Geronimo before his flight in two days. He and the dog had been inseparable since he found him in La Paz almost ten years before, but this mission was definitely not dog friendly. Ben thought this was a fairly good test for how shitty anything was. There seemed to be an inverse relationship with shittiness and dog friendliness. Geronimo's best option was the vet/vet/drug dealer, Bob. He and Geronimo made the short walk over to Bob's house on the oceanfront cliffs in La Jolla, Ben's backpack filled with a leash (almost never used), two dog bowls, food, and a brand new fuzzy toy shaped like a cow with a really long neck, bought by Ben out of guilt and sadness for leaving.

They knocked on the door, and Bob quickly opened it, a beer already in his hand for Ben. They walked inside, and Ben sat down and started on the beer.

"So..." Ben started.

"It is all good, man. Don't worry about it. As long as you need," Bob finished.

"You don't even know what I am going to ask," Ben protested.

"Dude, I can tell by the look on your face and your sad backpack full of dog stuff that your little FBI adventure is taking you someplace G-dog can't go, and can I watch him for you?" Bob explained.

"Yeah, that's it," Ben said, draining his beer, somewhat relieved he didn't have to ask.

"No problem, man. Happy to help out," Bob finished.

Ben felt instant relief as he looked out over the surf at Bird Rock (two to three feet, fair condition). "Thanks, man. I really appreciate it. This is definitely not how I planned to spend this month."

"Anytime," Bob replied easily.

Ben looked around the house again. Something tugged at his brain, but it was too full of other crap at the moment to figure out exactly what it was. There were the surfboards, which made sense. The military awards, honors, and photos from parts unknown—all good there. The pile of gear bags and Pelican cases by the door—explained last time. Ben took the next beer proffered and drowned his paranoia in some Mexican lager while watching the sun approach the horizon. Geronimo lay down at his feet and groaned in the sunlight streaming in through the window. Ben let his mind go blank in preparation for his trip. He hadn't noticed that Bob had left the room until he came back holding the latest Motorola sat phone.

"Take this," he said, holding it out with a charger.

"Man, you can just e-mail me anything about the dog," Ben said, confused.

"Not for that, dude. Just in case. You are going overseas, I assume. You mentioned undercover, I think. Based on my experience in Afghanistan, you never know when one of these will come in handy," Bob said, making good sense. There were many times in his life when Ben literally would have killed for a sat phone.

"That is an excellent point, my friend," he said, taking the phone and mentally adding it to his package of items for when things went seriously wrong. They sat there drinking, talking story in the way of surfers everywhere. Reminiscing about El Niño events of yore and comparing it to this one, mostly unfavorably. They made fun of Phil for his psychotic conspiracy theories and complimented his preternatural ability to ride a longboard beautifully in almost any conditions, big or small.

Ben left later that night. Geronimo seemed to know what was up and stayed behind without protest. Perhaps it was the beachfront location, but he seemed perfectly content to hang out at Bob's for the duration. Ben wandered along the shorefront in La Jolla and down to Pacific Beach, taking in the cool ocean air. He stopped at London's West End and put his hand on the door but quickly released it and kept walking. He wanted another drink to keep his demons at bay, but didn't want to talk to anyone. He thought it better just to make his way home. His freedom depended on his actions over the next week.

31

The next morning, Ben arose, mostly fresh; went for a run on the beach; returned to the apartment where dreams went to die; and took a shower. He sat on his crumbling concrete patio with a freshly made espresso, his dog's absence amplifying his normal cosmic loneliness. He sat for a long time feeling hollow but lethal. After his coffee, he went to his garage and locked it down with the deadbolts, motion sensors, and alarm, both inside and out. He couldn't care less about the apartment; he twisted the handle and stashed the keys in his yard in some silicone dog shit. He had some time before his flight, so he stopped by the barber. This was not a usual visit. Ben cut his hair about once every six months, his dark, shaggy curls an accurate representation of the beach bum he was. He had the barber cut it much shorter than usual, and he emerged looking more like the legitimate attorney he was claiming to be. He rolled an UberBLACK car to the airport where he was to meet SA Goodman for their flight. On the curb he saw the fed, standing in his rumpled cargo pants and Hawaiian shirt. Ben noticed the bulge of an ankle holster under his left pant leg. Goodman waved at Ben as he approached in his new suit and starched white shirt open at the collar. Ben nodded back. They made some small talk before going inside. At the counter, Howie checked them both in. The government rate had them both in center seats on a sold-out flight direct to Paris. Ben jumped in with his American Express to upgrade himself to first class. He told Howie that it was to make sure he remained in character and away from his handler if they were followed, but the truth was that it was just a small "fuck you" to the government that was holding him hostage. It didn't change the dynamic; it was purely symbolic, but at least the food would be better, and he could sleep comfortably in first class knowing how cramped Goodman would be in economy.

32

Iraq

In the bunker outside of Tikrit, flattering portraits of the Hussein family hung on concrete walls. A 1984 Rolls Royce Silver Spur with flat tires caught the light of a crystal chandelier. Three stories underground, General Qureshi studied his project as he sipped mint tea. His focus was in the center of the room under mobile floodlights. It was an early 2000s–era Xerox-brand photocopier. He felt momentarily ridiculous. He was a warrior; he should be in the field commanding troops and killing the enemy. But this was the big picture, the "thirty-thousand-foot view," as the Americans liked to say. There were plenty of people willing to go out and die in the desert for Allah, but few with the skills to put this deal together for the caliphate. He had to talk himself down like this three or four times a day. The copier was a test piece. Men in lab coats buzzed around it making final checks and tests in preparation for shipment to Italy. It was no ordinary photocopier, it was being specially modified by ISIS engineers to test the trigger Giancarlo Trentino was bringing to the meet. If it passed the test, then they would have a deal. Two million dollars for two hundred weapons-grade triggered spark gaps. The chief engineer looked over his shoulder and gave the general a thumbs-up. It was ready.

33

Charles de Gaulle Airport, Paris

Ben made his way through French Immigration and Customs. He spotted his HSI handler on the other side, and the man did not look good. Special Agent Goodman looked at Ben through half-closed eyes sunken deep in his head with large, dark circles underneath. He gave Ben a nod.

"You OK, man?" Ben asked, showing no ill effects from his first-class flight.

"No more screaming..." he mumbled in response.

"What?"

"Eleven hours. How can a kid scream for eleven hours? Has to be some kind of record. Let's get the fuck out of here."

"Roger," said Ben, collecting his gear.

They jumped on France's high-speed rail, the TGV, bound for Monaco. Ben upgraded them both to first class out of pity and ordered coffee. Goodman slept for about half an hour before perking up and getting down to business.

"OK, sport, here is the deal: We have alerted the police services of France, Monaco, and Italy to the situation, so we have backup if we need it. I just need you to feed me as much intel as possible, and we will respond. Unfortunately, it's going to be somewhat fast and loose since we don't even know if it's actually happening on this trip," Goodman explained.

"Backup sounds all well and good, but who are the primaries on this? Please don't tell me that it's just me and you."

"You got it, champ. We're going to have a light footprint this time. DHS didn't want to antagonize our allies by dropping a bunch of gun-toting feds in Europe. So, the way I hope it goes down is that you find out when and where the exchange is; you tell me; then I tell the locals, and they make the bust while we sit back and collect commendations, promotions, and accolades. Sound good?"

"Oh yeah. This can't fail."

"Tell me everything you can about these devices so that I can try and spot them in advance," Ben continued.

"Unfortunately, these triggers are pretty nondescript. They look like a small electronic squid, and they may be wrapped in some static free foil packaging. They are not explosive or otherwise dangerous on their own, but they are pretty easy to hide. The good news is that the deal is for two hundred of them, so you would probably need one or two duffel bags to carry them. That could be a key ID feature for you. Look out for Trentino or his people hauling any large bags; those could be the triggers."

"Or just their regular luggage."

"Correct."

"Or a bag of climbing gear?"

"Also correct."

"Piece of cake."

Ben grumbled irritably as he picked up his coffee and looked out the window at the French countryside whipping by at ninety miles per hour.

34

After about one hour, Ben received a text from Trentino that read, "Change of plans. Cancelled the suite. Go to harbor instead. Take a water taxi out. It is called The Nautilus, eighty-three feet, red hull, flying an American flag, should be easy to spot."

Ben showed the text message to his handler.

"This is great. If they make the deal on the boat, they can't run. I can just have the Italian Coast Guard stop them afterward and sew this whole thing up!" Goodman said with what Ben believed was a healthy dose of naïveté.

Agent Goodman had two rooms for them at the modestly priced Hotel Villa Boeri. After checking in, Ben mentally geared up for the operation. Once he lit the fuse on this deal, it could either fizzle out or blow up entirely. Ben walked the five minutes down the waterfront, dressed in his best high-dollar-lawyer-on-vacation outfit, and looked out across the harbor for the boat. It didn't take him long to spot it. It certainly wasn't the biggest yacht in the Monaco harbor, but it stood out nonetheless. Its hull was painted blood red, and it had the swept-back look of a speedboat; it just happened to be eighty-three feet long with pulsing electronica airing out over the water. The brand name on the side read, "Azimut." Ben had never seen anything like it in person. It looked like something a villain from a James Bond movie would own. Considering the circumstances, Ben thought that was entirely appropriate. He took a moment to collect himself and got into character. He ducked into one of the waterfront hotels and ordered a Kronenbourg at the bar. He could hear the wail of Formula One cars and took his drink outside. Ben didn't know what the rules in Monaco were for drinking on the street, but he figured that he would find out one way or another and walked outside. The race wasn't until tomorrow; today the teams were practicing. He watched as the multimillion-dollar pieces of high art and technology screamed past along the water's edge. Based on his recent experience on the track, he looked at them with a new appreciation and even some nascent smugness.

They don't even have to lean to turn.

He walked away from the sound of the race cars. He walked around the harbor until he found a dock with water taxis. Ben spoke virtually no French, so he just pointed toward the bay and said, "Azimut." The taxi driver spread his hands out and cocked his head quizzically. Ben hadn't noticed before that at least four of the giant yachts lying at anchor bore the brand Azimut.

"*Nautilus*," Ben said.

The boatman just squinted.

"*Avec la Musique!*" he said, exasperated and pointing impotently, using up most of his French acquired in one ten-day surf trip through Biarritz fifteen years earlier.

The driver isolated the proper Azimut and sped off.

He could feel the bass before he could actually hear it. He sped across the water toward the obscene yacht. A large party was going on at his destination with about a dozen high-dollar runabouts rafted up to it. The taxi pulled astern, where a few of the less inebriated partygoers tied up the old boat. Ben paid the driver and stepped up and through the transom to the large afterdeck. He was reminded of something his friend Joe had once told him, which was that you knew you were on a yacht instead of a regular boat if it didn't move when you came aboard. The *Nautilus* definitely didn't move. From somewhere in the crowd, a beer appeared in his hand, which he took without question. The party was in full swing, with revelers in every stage of dress and intoxication. There were the old, fat guys in suits who clearly had the means for such a vessel themselves all the way down to the semi-nude hangers on. Though fully dressed, Ben definitely put himself at the lower end of the spectrum. He was going to do his best to act his way up the chain. He approached a group of dancing women in bikinis and asked if they knew where Giancarlo was. He got a few head nods and fingers pointed forward. He found Giancarlo with his girlfriend, Sophia, in the main salon talking to a group of middle-aged guys of indeterminate ethnicity. Ben thought these guys could be the contacts for the sale of the triggers. On a closer look, Ben's intuition told him this was way too visible, and these guys looked way too Euro-douchey to be Islamic fundamentalists. Giancarlo's face quickly changed the subject on Ben's mind. He had two black eyes, a bandaged nose, and deep scrapes down one side of his cheek. Ben immediately thought of the loan sharks he knew who worked the beach in San Diego, but again, this explanation didn't really fit the scene.

"You made it, man!" Giancarlo shouted, a lopsided smile spreading across his face. He gave Ben a bear hug then clasped his shoulders. "This is so great. I'm glad you made it. You will love it. The race tomorrow is going to blow your mind! You remember Sophia?"

"Great to see you too, man. Thanks for having me. I have always wanted to see this race, and from a yacht. I mean…" said Ben in feigned speechlessness. "Nice to see you again as well, Sophia," he finished.

Sophia nodded to him with barely concealed contempt.

"What the fuck happened to your face, dude?" asked Ben, the first genuine thing he had said all day.

"El Cap, man. Soph and I were on pitch twenty-three, and I was leading it. I took a pretty big fall, and three pieces of gear popped. I swung about a hundred feet and smashed into the wall. I am lucky to be standing here. Sophia was more upset than I have ever seen her."

"Gear popped? Is that normal?" Ben asked.

"Not for me. I'm really anal about where and how I place protection. Never had a piece blow before. I think maybe my cams were getting old and worn. I want to check them out when I get back, but I can't find them. They disappeared in all the YOSAR chaos. Maybe my number was just up."

"YOSAR?"

"Sorry. Yosemite Search and Rescue. They rapped down to us to help me out of there. I might have been able to make it, but some people saw the fall from the ground and called up the helo, so I took the help rather than send them home. Which reminds me, I met a friend of yours under the Great Roof."

"Great Roof? Friend of mine? What are you talking about, man?"

"There is a big overhang on El Capitan called the Great Roof. It is a nice place to spend the night because of the cover from the weather. It's also a tough section, so it makes sense for climbing parties to stop there. We set up our porta-ledges there for the night with another party that started on the route before us. Cool dudes. Anyway, one of the guys in that party was a guy named Blair, ski patroller from Aspen, huge boozer, I liked him immediately. I'm not sure how your name came up, but he made sure to tell me that you were—and I want to get this right because he seemed pretty serious about it so I wrote it down—'one badass, righteous, brodacious motherfucker,'" Trentino read aloud from a page he had taken from his pocket.

Ben laughed a little too nervously, he thought. He wondered how much Blair had told him. His cover story was mostly true, but he wasn't sure if it would weather the tale that Blair had to tell, namely that the two of them had gone looking for a cartel plane crash full of dope in the Colorado mountains last year, resulting in the death of a few cartel sicarios and the seizure of several million dollars' worth of heroin by the FBI.

"Oh yeah, Blair and I went to high school together and reconnected last year on a ski trip to Aspen. Small world!" said Ben, hoping to paper over the thing as quickly as possible.

"That's exactly what he said," replied Giancarlo with a mischievous grin that made Ben wonder exactly what he knew.

"Let's go up to the flybridge and watch the practice laps. There is a great view from up there," Giancarlo suggested. The group in suits had by now dispersed without introduction and remained unknown. Ben, Giancarlo, and Sophia made their way upstairs. From the flybridge, one could see all of Monte Carlo Harbor and the section of racetrack that ran along the water. Ben nursed his beer, trying to keep straight for the job at hand. He tried to make small talk with Sophia with the purpose of gaining some insight into her relationship with Trentino and also because she was impossibly beautiful. She wasn't impressed with Ben and was not afraid to let that sentiment be known by her curt answers and general stoicism. Ben had a difficult time reading her. A woman who had no interest in him made perfect sense, but her hostility seemed like something different.

Is she jealous?

Did she think Ben was going to take away her plaything? That didn't seem right either. She had a predatory vibe but not in an appealingly sexual or seductive way. She had a hardness that didn't suit her surroundings and her arm-candy act. Ben let those thoughts get blown out of his head as the shriek from a Formula One car came blasting across the water. Giancarlo talked to Ben about the intricacies of F1 racing, the history of the track, the drivers, and the rest of it. Ben feigned interest for the sake of his cover, nodding when appropriate. In his head, Ben was running through his interactions thus far, hoping to glean some sort of clue as to when this deal was going down. He needed something he could feed to Goodman so he could get out of here and go the fuck home. He looked down at a group of girls on the afterdeck dancing to electronic dance music in their bikinis. He leaned over and earnestly asked Sophia if she thought what they were listening to was house music, trance music, or good old-fashioned techno music. He thought he saw the trace of a smile as she responded with a sound like *pfffffff* before walking away and heading downstairs herself. Ben paused for a while, taking in the sea air before realizing that his act was going to require more drinking to blend in and loosen up. He climbed down the ladder and worked his way past the dancing girls and into the main salon, where he saw the suited guys from earlier lining up a big rail of cocaine. Ben flinched then regained his composure and grabbed a beer from the galley.

35

He spent the afternoon with one eye on the practice race and one eye on Giancarlo. Wandering around the yacht and looking at the Mediterranean coastline, Ben imagined that had he gone into law like the family had wanted and stayed back east, it wouldn't have been out of the question that he could have ended up at this very same party, but as a different person—a fatter corporate lawyer, guest of one of the legit partygoers rather than an FBI asset trying to foil an international conspiracy to put nuclear-weapons technology in the hands of a Middle Eastern death cult. He added it all up and decided that all things being equal, he rather preferred where he had landed, threat of jail and all. He laughed out loud at how absurd it was. A lithe girl in her mid-twenties in an evening gown slit up the side looked over and asked with a generic American accent what he was laughing at. Ben responded truthfully that he was just laughing at how life had turned out. She looked around at the yacht and the ocean and had to agree before slinking off through the crowd. Ben drank enough beer to keep him in the party, but not so much that he lost his meager investigative edge. As the sun started to sink in the sky, race practice finished, and the party wound down. Ben thought he might get a chance to pry into Trentino's brain a little bit. He was wrong. He watched as Trentino went into the main cabin with a sense of purpose. When he reemerged, he had changed into athletic gear and tennis shoes. In his hand he carried an aluminum-shelled attaché case. The sort of thing that in a bad movie would be handcuffed to someone's wrist. He flagged down a passing water taxi, which then pulled up to the platform.

"Hey, man, where are you headed?" Ben asked, trying like the devil to appear nonchalant.

"I have some business over the border in Italy. No big deal; I will be back in a couple of hours. Help yourself to whatever you want. Mi yacht es su yacht," he said.

Ben went for broke. "Cool. Thanks. Hey, what's in the case, dude?"

"You really don't know?" he asked.

Ben shook his head with a drag on his beer.

"It's a McGuffin, you tool. Everybody wants it." And with an impish grin, Trentino quickly jumped on the boat and sped away toward shore.

Ben bristled. Was this guy fucking with him be-cause he knew he was FBI or just in a general way? Didn't matter. He had to move. Now. The bag seemed too small for all the triggers, but he thought maybe he was going to pick them up someplace else. Either way, Ben had to follow. He waited until Trentino was far enough away before searching frantically for a way to follow him. The American girl he had shared a laugh with earlier was just climbing into a navy-blue-and-crimson Chris Craft runabout. Ben leaned over and asked for a ride.

"Sure, jump in," she said with a smile. "Where are you headed?"

"To the shore, same place as that water taxi," Ben said, indicating the boat headed away from them.

"Are you following that guy?" she said coyly.

"Total coincidence."

"Sure it is," she said, continuing to grin and push-ing the throttle forward. "So it is OK if I just follow right behind them, then?"

"I would prefer you didn't," Ben said, knowing he was busted and hoping he hadn't just burned the whole operation.

"Don't worry, secret agent man. I won't tell." She smiled.

Ben sat back to enjoy the awkward ride. His pilot did an excellent job of keeping the water taxi in sight but at a discreet distance, even using other anchored yachts as cover. Whoever this chick was, she would make an excellent fed. The water taxi landed at a public dock, and Ben watched as Trentino paid and got out. Without prompting, Ben's new partner pulled up at a second public dock nearby. Close, but not too close.

"Here ya go. Good luck," she said, winking.

Casting off his normal surliness, Ben leaned over, kissed her full on the mouth, and said, "Thanks."

He alighted onto the dock and ducked behind the cabin of a commercial fishing boat just as Giancarlo looked across the water in his direction. He then turned away and walked quickly toward the city. Ben's ride motored off with a wave, and he was on his own. Ben stayed back and fired off a text to Goodman that they were on the move as Trentino made his way over the now quiet racetrack and toward the Grand Casino. In the real world of law-enforcement investigations, you would never try a single-man foot surveillance. It is too easy to get burned, to lose the subject, but that was exactly what Ben was doing. He was starting to feel really strung out, but it also felt galvanizing. He lived only in this moment; there was no past or future, only this. He lurked from building to building, trying his best not to get spotted by his target nor look so whacky that the Monaco police would notice him. He wondered how this was going to work in the casino when Trentino cruised right past it and took a left down Boulevard de Suisse. He tracked Trentino for a few blocks and was relieved that he seemed not to be attempting any countersurveillance. This was good news. Ben knew that his one-man show would not survive even the most rudimentary tradecraft if Trentino knew to do it. Ben followed as he made his way to the Gare de Monaco. Trentino bought a ticket and slid up to the platform. Luckily for Ben, the station was crowded because of the race and provided good cover. After about fifteen minutes, a train rolled in bound for Milano. Giancarlo looked around the platform, then got into the first-class car. Ben sat on the platform to make sure it wasn't a fake-out, then jumped in the car immediately behind first class as the train rolled out.

36

As the train headed east and the sun went down, Ben kept his eyes on the doorway to the next car. When the conductor came by, Ben bought a ticket all the way to Milan, having no idea if or when Giancarlo was getting off. It was possible there might be a meeting between Trentino and his buyer on the train, but since he clearly didn't have the triggers with him yet, it wasn't worth the risk of getting made by going up to first class. At every stop along the Riviera, Ben got up and went to the door so he could follow Trentino if he saw him getting off, and every time he didn't get off, Ben wearily returned to his seat, waiting in tension. Before long they crossed into Italy. At San Remo, Ben made his normal move toward the door, trying to look nonchalant to the other passengers. This time he spotted Trentino on the platform. He hit the button to open the door and waited.

Trentino was looking at his phone. If Ben jumped off now, there was a good chance he would be seen by his target. The seconds crept by. Trentino looked up and started walking away just as the doors moved to close; Ben jammed his hand through at the last second, and the doors responded. One of the passengers shook her head at his antics. Ben smiled at the old woman and jumped off.

He followed as Trentino made his way through the city. Like much of old Europe, San Remo was dense with buildings, the roads and walkways narrow. It was a good place for foot surveillance, lots of cover. Trentino and his tail navigated the maze of the medieval city, Trentino periodically checking his phone until he approached a small bar. Ben posted up across the street in an alley as Trentino went inside. Ben had a good view inside the corner windows of the business, and he could still hide among the detritus in the alley. He crouched among the boxes and watched as Trentino met with someone who appeared to be an older Middle Eastern man. They sat in the window chatting over coffee. Trentino put the attaché case on the counter and opened it. He pulled out a single item. All Ben could tell was that it was small and black. It had to be what he was looking for. Trentino replaced the object in the case, and the two moved to leave the bar. They walked out into the night together, Ben following at a distance as they worked their way farther into the warren of alleys that make up the city. Eventually, they approached the open roll-up door of an old brick warehouse, the light from inside barely illuminating the cobblestone. The two men walked inside. Ben angled over bit by bit, slicing the pie, trying to get a look inside without being spotted. He eventually got a look at the two men standing around what appeared to be a copy machine in an otherwise empty warehouse. Ben was tired, stressed, and now confused. He decided not to try to make any sense of it but to be as good of a witness as possible and report back to the feds what went down.

Ben watched as the old Arab opened the side of the copy machine and held out his palm. Giancarlo put the trigger into his hand and stepped back. The warrior then inserted the device into the guts of the machine and powered it up. Ben panicked for a moment as he realized he might be about to bear very close witness to the mother of all suicide bombings. He had the fleeting instinct to run, but with even his rudimentary knowledge of nuclear weapons, he knew the silliness of that idea. He exhaled as the general fired up the copy machine and made a single copy of whatever was on the plate. The old guy smiled broadly and shook Trentino's hand vigorously. Ben had just relaxed a bit when he saw movement out of the corner of his eye. He looked to his left and saw what appeared to be a long silencer attached to the end of a rifle barrel sticking out between the stacks of pallets in the alley. On instinct Ben flew into motion. He picked up a pallet and ran over to the gunman and slammed it down hard on the weapon. A bullet cracked into a masonry wall as Ben felt a foot come from space and drill him right in the face. He staggered backward as an elbow drilled him in the other side of his face. Before he could recover, his assailant grabbed both of his lapels and hissed, "You fucking idiot."

He recognized the perfume and the voice as that of Sophia, Giancarlo's future ex-girlfriend. Ben's bell had been rung pretty hard, and he was trying to pull himself together as she continued, "You have no idea how fucked you are."

Ben finally snapped out of it and kneed her in the vulva as hard as he could. Her immediate response was a loud *oooof* as she staggered backward. She turned around clumsily, coughing as Ben pulled himself to-gether. Sophia lurched toward the assault rifle lying farther down the alley. Ben saw her move and charged her as hard as he could from behind, slamming with the full force of his weight, pushing her past the gun and out of the alley and into the street. The rear tires of the bus locked up as she hit the grille with the sound of a porterhouse hitting concrete. Ben saw the terrified faces of the fat tourists in the window as the bus ground to a halt on top of the former assassin. He quickly grabbed the rifle and looked back toward the warehouse. The door was closed and its occupants presumably long gone. Thinking this was a good plan, Ben bolted down the alley away from the gruesome scene. He made his way from shadow to shadow, trying to conceal the rifle under his jacket. He had pulled the silencer and put it into his pocket, substantially reducing the length of the weapon. He made his way through the darkness to the water and walked out onto a long wooden pier. He sat down on the end of the pier, trying to look like one more drunk guy lamenting something and hoping the ocean would provide an answer. Somewhat confident that he wasn't being watched, he dumped the rifle into the water, noting that it was a nice M4 as it slipped under the waves. Who supplied that piece of hardware? The silencer followed. Ben sat for a moment and noticed there was actually a nice swell running. Through the darkness he could hear waves exploding onto the breakwater around the harbor. It was a particularly stark contrast. In the abstract, he could have spent the night planning a Mediterranean surf session for tomorrow instead of making roadkill out of an assassin.

Ben dragged himself to his feet and used his handkerchief to dab at the blood on his face as he made his way down the pier back to the waterfront. From the outside, he looked like he was holding it together, but Ben was having a hard time connecting all the dots.

Who the fuck was Sophia? Who was she working for?

Ben tidied up as much as possible and started looking for a way out of there. He flagged down a cab, and although his Italian was every bit as bad as his French, he made it clear that they were headed to Monte Carlo. The driver shot him a questioning glance, at which point Ben held out a wad of euros. This seemed to answer the question, and they sped off in the Fiat diesel. After about an hour, they crossed back into Monaco, and Ben pointed the driver toward his hotel. He stopped him two blocks away as a precaution. He paid the driver, watched him leave, then made his way back to his budget digs.

A very frazzled-looking Goodman opened the door when Ben knocked. An equally jacked Ben Adams slipped into the room and went straight to the minibar, where he cracked a small bottle of vodka and downed it. Goodman opened his laptop, hands poised, and said, "Well, what happened?"

Ben explained while Special Agent Goodman dutifully typed up his case report based on Ben's recollection. He stopped typing when Ben got to the part about shoving Giancarlo's girlfriend in front of a bus. He looked at Ben pensively for a few moments, then shut the computer.

"Say that again," he said, almost whispering.

Ben went through it again, including everything from the copier to the murder, the M4, and the surf.

"Let's leave that alone for the moment, shall we? I have a lot of calls to make, and you look like shit. Go to your room, get some sleep, and let's meet again in the morning, around eight? I'll have breakfast brought up. Sound good, buddy?" he said like one would to a child who was in dire need of a nap.

Ben jutted his chin upward in agreement, went back to the minibar, grabbed a handful of the tiny liquor bottles, and left the room without a word.

37

Ben awoke not knowing where he was. As the room came into focus, he remembered everything and sighed. He wasn't going to work today. He was calling in sick. He replayed the previous night's events in his head. That didn't help. He had killed people before, but by and large they had all had it coming. Last night, he had reacted instinctively. He wasn't trying to kill anyone. He was trying to stop an assassin. The problem was that it was an assassin who seemed to be trying to rid the world of some potentially very bad dudes. So what did that make him? He dumped that thought for the moment and imagined how he would spend the day. He wondered if he could rent a surfboard from a surf shop in Monte Carlo and how long the swell he saw last night in Italy would last. His thoughts of surfing died with the knock at the door. In an act of spite, Ben answered it completely naked. Special Agent Goodman marched in with a sense of purpose. He dropped a binder on the table and walked over to the coffee machine and went to work getting a brew on. He made no mention of Ben's nudity.

"OK, boyo, this is another one of those good-news– bad-news situations," he started.

Ben, still nude, said nothing and sat down slowly at the table. He waited with his palm to his forehead for the next event. Goodman sat down and got to it.

"At this point the Italian police are treating this like an accident. Privately, they are saying that it looks like sui- cide, but they're keeping the lid on that out of respect for the family, which has yet to be notified. You did a great job of cleaning that up, by the way. This could have been one heck of an international incident."

"Is that the good news or the bad news?" Ben said, exhaling.

"The good. The bad news is that I think we know who she was. I have some friends on the dark side who told me that your friend Sophia is Mossad. Was Mossad. Sorry."

"What the fuck was she doing?"

"The same thing that we are, but she was doing it in a more…how should we call it? Israeli fashion? They are very proactive. Their policy is to pretty much eliminate every potential threat and worry about ev- erything else later. They call it 'mowing the lawn,' which reminds me, I got a call from one of my friends at the Park Service. Apparently the odds of Giancarlo's climbing accident on El Capitan actually being an accident are pretty long. Sophia probably tried to take him out discreetly, high up in the mountains with no witnesses, *Eiger Sanction* style, but he survived the attempt, so she dialed up the effort to include an M4. You have to admire the efficiency of it."

"So I should have just let her do her job, then?" Ben asked, eyes staring unfocused across the room.

"Not necessarily there, champ. They have their priorities, and we have ours. It was just a case of bad luck and a lack of deconfliction."

Ben shuddered when he heard that word. A lack of deconfliction was what had put him in the can for five years and cost a good agent his life. It didn't sound any better now with some age on it.

"Either way, it doesn't change our plan. Your cover is probably intact. The deal is still going down at some place and time that we don't know yet. Your job is to find out when and where," he lectured. "Sound good?"

"Sounds terrific."

"Drink some coffee, and get dressed. I'm having some breakfast sent up to your room, and after you eat and pull yourself together, you get back out to that boat and back to work. *Capisce?*"

"Yeah, yeah. OK," Ben said, standing to refill his coffee, his penis at eye level with the hardworking civil servant. Goodman recoiled in his chair until Ben sat back down again.

"OK, I'm out. Good job. Keep at it. You're doing great!" he said with the fake enthusiasm usually found in quarterly sales meetings in the timeshare business.

38

Ben pouted in his room for about an hour after breakfast before finally pulling himself together. He dressed up again, trying to simulate the rich-lawyer-on-vacation motif. He strolled down to the docks with his coffee, trying to imagine he was doing something else with his time. He hired the same water taxi from yesterday and thought that maybe the boat driver was looking at him suspiciously. *Probably paranoia*, he thought and kept his cool. On the way out to the *Nautilus*, Ben noticed neither pulsing dance music nor a raft of expensive boats tied up to it. It seemed eerily quiet. He paid the driver and stepped onto the rear deck of the megayacht.

"Heeello?" he shouted into the boat. No response.

After last night's shenanigans, Ben wasn't about to take any chances. He slowly took down the boat room by room, the way he would have on a search warrant, but this time alone, unarmed, with no backup. He quick-peeked all the corners and worked methodically. By the time he reached the door of the master stateroom, he had cleared the entire rest of the ship except for the engine room. In the master he spotted Giancarlo Trentino facedown on the bed, shirtless and not moving. Ben walked over to the bed to check for a pulse. As he put his hand on the neck of the dead man, he felt and heard the body move. He jumped back as Trentino turned his head toward Ben, apparently unhurt but upset.

"Look at this man," he said, thrusting out a crumpled sheet of paper.

Ben took the sheet and read it. It was handwritten in very beautiful cursive and purported to be from Sophia. It was a standard-issue Dear John letter explaining that she was going back to North Carolina to be with her mother and "sort out some things." Ben blinked hard as he imagined a group of Mossad operators quickly forging this letter and getting it on the boat last night in the time after Sophia had been smooshed but before Trentino had come back from his meeting. Their efficiency impressed and terrified him.

"I don't think I have ever been so unceremoniously dumped before," Trentino said, sitting up. "I didn't even know that she was from North Carolina."

Ben remained silent. His acting skills were being pushed to their limits, so he thought it best to let Trentino run this train of thought down on his own.

"Did I blow it? Could she have been the one?" he asked; Ben hoped rhetorically. "Well? Ben?"

It was not rhetorical, but fortunately Ben could answer this one with absolute sincerity. "I very seriously doubt that she was the one for you, man."

"What a fucked-up deal. She was supposed to help me at my next race."

"What race?" Ben asked, initially not caring but suddenly realizing this might be important.

"When I met you at Laguna Seca, I was tuning up for a race at Kyalami in South Africa in a couple of weeks. I think I have a shot at a podium place, but I need some help with the pits, the bike, et cetera. Sophia was my gal."

Ben flushed. This was his opening; he could get the feds what they wanted, but he had to play it right to be believable.

"I can do it. I can help. I have a few court appearances coming up, but they're easy. I can farm them out to some of my colleagues," Ben said, nearly cracking up when he imagined his "colleagues": Phil, the paranoid longboarder; or Jose, the guy he bought his breakfast and coffee from; or Bob, his vet/weed dealer/dog sitter. He kept it together and sent the delivery smoothly.

"That's perfect. You'll do it?" Trentino asked hopefully, apparently fully recovered from the loss of the love of his life.

"Gian, fair warning, I am not a mechanic."

"Dude, you don't need to be. The bike is in tip-top shape. The tires will last the entire race. I just need someone to help me with the logistics—arranging the stuff, helping me organize, that kind of thing. My treat! South Africa has some good climbing, easy stuff that you can cut your teeth on. I'll bring my gear, and after the race we can get out in the bush and really get after it!"

Ben was having a hard time deciding whether this guy was a great actor or if he was really this stoked about motorcycle racing and climbing.

Maybe a bit of both.

"Tell you what. As crew, I'll give you twenty-five percent of whatever I win at the race."

"How much is the top prize?" Ben asked, waiting for the punch line.

"About ten thousand US."

"My end is twenty-five hundred bucks? I have always wanted to surf South Africa. I am totally in," said Ben truthfully.

"Bravo!" His broken heart totally healed. "Thanks, man. I mean it. I might have a shot at a decent career here," Trentino continued by way of additional unnecessary explanation.

Ben noticed that Trentino hadn't specified the nature of the potential career as he thought about his own role in all of this.

"Let's go have a drink and get ready for the start of the race," Trentino finished, getting up and getting dressed.

They moved upstairs and went to the bar in the main salon. Giancarlo threw down two rocks glasses and dropped in a couple of extra-large ice cubes. The mark of the true drinker, the cubes were designed for maximum ice and minimum surface area to resist melting and thus diluting the precious booze. He poured some expensive rye whiskey over the ice and handed Ben a glass.

"To South Africa!" he said as they clinked glasses.

Ben nodded assent, and they went outside to the rear deck. From the shore they could hear a reverse countdown beginning in French. They hustled up to the flybridge to see the start of the race. Ben wasn't much of a sports spectator, but even he was impressed when $1 billion worth of cars tore away from the start line and ripped through downtown Monte Carlo.

Ben worked his drink over, then climbed downstairs and returned with another. Smaller boats started tying up to the *Nautilus*, with spectators boarding and heading straight to the bar. Ben saw his opportunity to speak alone with the bad guy slipping, so he went for some more intel.

"Tell me about your company, man," he said, trying and failing to seem as cool as possible.

"It's a pretty simple deal. I run an electronics design-and-manufacturing firm that my dad started. We make all sorts of complicated little things for consumer, medical, and military applications," he said, eyes locked across the harbor watching the little cars zoom by.

"You can just do that? Military stuff, I mean?" Ben prodded, trying not to be obvious.

"Sure. There's a process just like anything else, but most military hardware is made by private companies. The most obvious are the aircraft companies like Boeing and Lockheed, et cetera. If you want to sell outside the U.S. it is a whole mess of regulations— the International Traffic in Arms Regulations, the Trading with the Enemy Act, or tweeeeah, as we call it—and you need a license from the State Department, but if you can do all of that, you can make some decent money," he said, still distracted by the race. Ben wished that he were wearing a wire.

"Outside the United States? Like who, for example?"

"Foreign governments usually, ostensibly our allies," he said with a mouthful of rye and ice. "The worst part," he continued without prodding, "is that for a lot of it, it is paid for with foreign aid. The two biggest recipients of US foreign aid are Israel and Egypt, and surprise, surprise, they are the two biggest customers of US military hardware. It is like welfare for defense contractors...Don't look at me like that. It is fucked up; I know, but it is the system. What are you going to do?" he said, shrugging and heading down the ladder for another drink.

Ben let that sink in as he watched the race. He heard Trentino making small talk on the main deck as he made his way to the bar. Ben didn't really pay much attention to foreign affairs except for how it related to surf trips he planned but never took. The foreign aid/defense contractor rabbit hole was not something he was interested in getting into at the moment. He compartmentalized it and focused on the task at hand: stop the deal, and stay out of jail.

When Trentino made his way back up top, Ben let him collect himself before getting back to it.

"So, do you like the work?" Ben asked, still digging.

"Not really. It was my dad's deal. I am looking to put together a few more big contracts and retire to focus on racing. In fact, that is what the meeting yesterday was about. I have a pretty good–size sale coming up."

"Cool. What are you selling?"

"Sorry, bud. Need to know. Lots of my deals are classified government stuff, so I can't really talk about it, but I promise you, it's boring stuff. Not like racing… Look at that shit! Raikkonen's Ferrari went for the pass on the inside of Hamilton in the Mercedes. Ballsy, man!" he shouted, pointing at the shore, excited like a little kid. After a minute he calmed down a bit and said, "Electronics just pays the bills while I figure out how to spend the rest of my life motorcycle racing and climbing." The sentiment sounded uncomfortably familiar to Ben.

Ben was drained from his undercover act, so he spent the rest of the day legitimately watching the race and getting quite drunk. He spotted the American girl with the Chris Craft from yesterday down below. She looked up at him and winked. Ben flinched; he was too burned to try to figure out if she was a spook, a fed, another assassin, or just some girl. Once again Ben's world seemed like a hall of mirrors. The rye helped him feel better about it, but it also limited his intellectual ability to deal. He kept drinking through to the end of the race then made his way down to an unoccupied stateroom and passed out in his suit.

39

Ben woke up feeling disjointed, as was now usual. He felt the rocking of the boat and remembered where he was. Giancarlo had told him he was heading back to the United States today before flying straight from San Francisco to South Africa for the race. Ben was pleased he could at least go home now but bummed out that he was almost certainly on the hook for the trip to South Africa. He left the stateroom and made his way to the galley. The refrigerator door was open, and a young woman wearing nothing but a long T-shirt was rooting around inside. The bottom of her near perfect rear end was just showing from under the shirt. She emerged with some cheese, a tomato, and a baguette. It was his boat driver who had winked at him the night before. She put the baguette in her mouth and used her free hand to shut the refrigerator. She walked by Ben, offering up her hand for a high five. Ben obliged with a loud slap, and without a word she disappeared into Giancarlo's master stateroom.

Ben looked around for the items necessary to assemble some form of coffee. He found an American-style coffee machine and got to work. He leaned against the counter while the brewing process worked its magic. His hand landed on a piece of paper. He picked it up and looked at it. It was a business card on thick but poor-quality paper with uneven edges. It was like the business card of someone starting a home-based business selling birdhouse-construction franchises. There had obviously been a large sheet of cards that had been cut out individually by hand. The face of it was framed by two crude black-and-white American flags. In the center was a name, "Bruce Brown, National Projects," and a phone number.

Ben blinked hard at the card. Bruce Brown was a surf filmmaker famous for having made *The Endless Summer* in 1963. This was definitely not his card. Something about the design bothered Ben. It was very simple and amateurish, but he had seen it before. He just couldn't remember where. The coffee pinged that it was finished. Ben slipped the business card into his pocket and went for the sweet rejuvenation of caffeine. He went on deck with his coffee to evaluate his circumstances and the decisions that had put him there. He inhaled the salt air as he looked down at his wrinkled suit and then over the water at the Monte Carlo skyline. He was definitely way off the reservation. He left the cup on the deck and flagged down a passing water taxi. He texted Giancarlo that he would see him stateside in a week. He went back to his budget digs on land where he found an increasingly strung out–looking Case Agent Goodman. Ben, finally calm himself, explained the situation about South Africa and how he thought it was likely a cover for the deal that would happen there. He made a lame attempt to get out of it, but both he and Goodman knew he was committed. They booked two tickets back to San Diego for that evening and packed their bags.

40

C urbside in San Diego, Ben Adams was looking fresh once again from first-class treatment
at the front of the plane, and Special Agent
Goodman in equal measure depleted from coach class
and its attendant discomforts. They parted ways, and
Goodman went straight to the local HSI office downtown to work on his case reports and give his superiors
in Washington and the FBI an update. Afterward, he
found a hotel nearby and went to sleep, knowing that
when he woke up he would be working his ass off to
get the operations in South Africa spun up. The special agent in charge of the HSI office in San Diego
had set him up with a desk and access to the systems
he would need for the duration of the op. The SAC
told Goodman that he remembered Ben Adams from
his early days on the FBI Joint Terrorism Task Force,
and although he had liked him well enough in the old

pre-prison days, Ben's current reputation did him no favors. The SAC figured this operation was one huge clusterfuck waiting to happen. But nobody had asked his opinion thus far, and the honchos in Washington wanted the op to go, so he let Goodman do his job.

Ben drove directly to the oceanfront home of Bob the vet/vet/drug dealer to collect Geronimo. The dog was clearly very glad to see him, and they chased and wrestled for a few minutes in the front yard before going in to thank Bob for his help. Ben knocked on the door. From inside the house came the call that it was open. Ben let himself in and found Bob relaxing on his couch watching a surf movie. He was so obviously splayed out and drinking that Ben thought for a second that it seemed forced. He disregarded that thought as he realized he had never seen Bob just hanging out before. He was always in motion: surfing, practicing animal medicine, whatever. His efficiency was total. To see him on the couch watching a movie was new. Ben grabbed a beer from the refrigerator without being offered one and sat down.

He noticed they were now watching Bruce Brown's *The Endless Summer*. Ben flashed back to the Bruce Brown business card from Monaco. He shook his head to rid himself of that thought as he took a big drink of his beer. The film followed a couple of surfers as they went around the globe, and at the part where they went to South Africa, Ben realized he wasn't going to get away from his impending trip, not even in his mind. He leaned in and said, "Bob, what does it take to bring a dog into another country?"

"Depends on the country," he said without looking.

"Like South Africa, for example."

"Easy, just a record of vaccinations and a letter from your vet, me, that the dog is healthy. Why? You going to Jeffreys for the Billabong Pro?"

"Something like that," Ben replied.

"When do you go?"

"About a week. Can you get that paperwork together for me?"

"No problem. Will have it tomorrow for ya."

"Thanks, man. I appreciate it."

"No problem. You will need G-dog to watch out for you over there. Remember, keep your powder dry, and hang on to that sat phone that I gave you for your other trip."

"A-firm," Ben replied, maintaining the alpha-male language but not escalating it.

They made small talk about the waves (three to five feet with Santa Ana conditions) and finished a few more beers and the movie before Ben rolled home with his dog and a good buzz. He was back in his zone. Happiness wasn't exactly Ben's bag, but this was as close as he could get.

He fished out the keys to his apartment from the phony dog turd in the unkempt lawn and worked the rusty door handle until the door creaked opened. Geronimo went in first, Ben right behind him. He was met with the musty smell of old beach construction, forever slightly moist and associated with the easy life at the beach. He dropped his bag and slid over to the door leading to the garage. He flipped open the cover to the keypad, which was made to look like a light switch but in fact operated nothing. He typed in his code, which was his former inmate number at Pelican Bay, and the security door cracked open. He hit the lights inside, and the garage became as bright as one of the biotech R and D facilities San Diego was becoming famous for. In fact, the guy who had helped him build out the space had designed the security system at the lab where the human genome was first sequenced. He walked around his garage. The wetsuits were dry. The surfboards were all lined up by height, looking very much like an arsenal, ready. He ran his hand down his old Jeep CJ-7. It was the first thing he had bought out of prison, and it had served him well. He noticed the battery tender blinking green, indicating a full charge. He walked over to the toolbox and opened it. Under an oily rag, he found his recent purchase: a nearly untraceable handgun. Modeled on a Glock, all the lower parts had been made on a 3-D printer out of a strong polymer. The barrel, slide, and spring were all bought legally and, since they didn't qualify as a firearm on their own, did not have serial numbers that could be traced and did not need to be registered. He put his hand around the grip and felt reassured by his knowledge of how to operate it. He had a mixed history with handguns: they had put him in jail, saved his life, and helped him end several others'. Whatever misgivings he had, he definitely appreciated their simple effectiveness. There wasn't anything ambivalent about a handgun; it had but one use. He dropped the magazine, ejected the round in the chamber, and disassembled the weapon. He reversed the process, charged a round in place, and returned the gun to the toolbox.

He decided to take a walk with G-dog around the beach and get a cup of coffee. He and the dog cruised down to the pier where he hit his favorite coffee stand and made some small talk with the owner, Dave, who regularly surfed the Point with Ben. To Ben, it seemed a lifetime ago since they had spoken, but to Dave, only the tides had gone in and out; he hadn't even noticed that Ben had been out of town. He found this reassuring and unsettling in equal measures, like the abyss was staring back. He sat down on the deck fronting the boardwalk where Geronimo loved to watch the walkers, bicyclists, skateboarders, and other dogs cruise by. Ben didn't judge; he enjoyed it as well. He watched the surfers out by the end of the pier, mentally noting each ride and where the waves broke. He hardly ever surfed there, but he would catalog what he saw for reference.

Overhearing snippets of conversation, Ben was becoming aware that the beach was abuzz with news that a reality-television star with a penchant for petty vengeance had just won the US presidential election. Ben pondered the implications of what that would mean for the country. Ben's own life tilted toward the surreal on its own, but the departure from reality now seemed to have spread to nationwide. He reaffirmed that he had been right to check out of society ten years ago and that he hadn't really been missing anything if this was what the voters were up to. Further, in relation to his current situation, if he failed...

Maybe who cares if there are a few extra nuclear weapons in the world?

Since, on balance, the world might not be worth saving, anyway. He processed this as he finished his coffee and scratched Geronimo on the head. He ultimately decided that the global implications of the new president were moot. Personally, he was still looking down the barrel of a long prison sentence if he didn't play ball with the feds. He was still certainly bound for South Africa in a few days, and in fact, under the totality of the circumstances, the best place to disappear for a while might have been the nuclear weapon–free southern hemisphere. The end of the continent of Africa might just have been what the doctor ordered. As long as he had some cash and Geronimo, Ben could probably hack it anywhere. Satisfied, he enjoyed his coffee for a while and let his thoughts return to surf.

After staring at the ocean for about an hour, he finally broke. He couldn't take it anymore; he had to paddle out. He took Geronimo home and got his nine-o Hobie and walked down to Tourmaline. It wasn't the best wave on the planet, but it had history, and the crowd was mellow. He paddled out into the lineup and nodded to some of the regulars he knew by face. The water temp was in the low sixties, the air temp about seventy with just a hint of offshore breeze. He turned toward the beach and paddled for a set wave. He was in position, and the others held back. It was a nice, clean, waist-high wave. Ben bottom-turned and then walked up to the nose for a quick cheater five, backed off to center, and then kicked out the back as the wave closed out onshore. That was the stuff. This was who he was. He paddled back out and surfed the same wave over and over again until sunset. He stripped down his wetsuit to waist level and rinsed off at the showers. Walking back through the parking lot toward home, he saw Phil loading up his van with one of his Skip Frye longboards.

Phil noticed him. "Hey, man. Where you been? I'm headed to the West End in about an hour. You want to go?" he said, apparently harboring no grudge related to the Daisy incident.

Two hours ago, Ben would have shrunk away from Phil, his dark conspiracy theories blending a little too easily with Ben's actual conspiracies, but after the surf, he was feeling good and agreed to meet him, and he was actually looking forward to it. He went home and hung his wetsuit up to dry in the garage, a special bucket underneath it to catch the drips and keep the floor of the garage pristine. He went to his nearly barren cupboard and took out a packet of ramen. Thrown down on the counter, the ramen waited for the water to boil while Ben put on a pair of jeans and a surf shop T-shirt then sat down at his computer. Going through his e-mail, there was only one of any relevance among the junk. It was from Jessica.

Dude, what the fuck is wrong with you? You have a shot at happiness in paradise. Don't blow it, I won't wait forever.

Ben thought she might have had a point. He tapped out a quick reply, which for him constituted a veritable emotional outpouring: **You may be right, I have made a mistake. I am into something strange right now at the behest of the government, but if I can get clear of it, G-dog and I will be back ASAP! Thanks for not giving up on me, it means a lot.**

He then typed, **I Love You.**

Then quickly deleted it and hit send. He had meant it, as much as he was capable at this point, but didn't want to freak her out. He threw the ramen into the pot and waited. Noticing the empty dog bowl, he sorted out Geronimo as well. Ben mowed through his ramen and went down to the West End where Phil was already holding court. Ben was still feeling good from the surf and his decision to return to New Zealand, so Phil's weirdness wasn't bothering him. He just sat down and enjoyed the show. Phil's rant du jour was related to the presidential election, and as far as Ben could tell, the gist of it was that while Phil was no fan of the new president, there was apparently ample reason to believe that his opponent had been using a DC-area pizza shop as a front for child sex trafficking to a remote Caribbean island, where America's rich and powerful used them as sex slaves under the protection of the FBI. Ben wondered aloud if the new president qualified as the rich and powerful in that scenario and said as well that he hadn't heard anything about this from his contacts in the FBI. Phil made eye contact for a brief moment and then quickly resumed his tale, citing "anonymous, high-placed sources." This was batshit crazy even for Phil, but Ben let it ride, drank his beers, and continued to watch. Later on, he played a few games of pool with one of his neighbors, an attractive, heavily tattooed girl who worked the bar at one of the trendier Pacific Beach hangouts Ben usually avoided. They flirted a bit before Ben tilted back toward the bar where Phil was still rattling away. Ben got his tab, paid it, and turned out through the door into the night. He was a little drunk, surfed up, and feeling good. He schlepped home and fell asleep in his chair watching *Magnum P.I.* on Netflix.

41

en woke to pounding on his door. He knew who it was and what he wanted and had hoped to pretend for a little while longer that things were going to be OK, but such was life. He was still in a good-enough mood from the last few days to harass his visitor some more. Ben opened the door stark naked again, exposing his hairy manliness to Special Agent Goodman, who reeled at the sight and stumbled back a step.

"C'mon, man, why?" he pleaded, Geronimo barking in apparent agreement.

Ben laughed aloud and motioned him in, walking to the bedroom to get some board shorts on, then went to the kitchen to get some caffeine out of his espresso maker. Goodman was in the kitchen unfolding what by now had become a very large case file. Geronimo lay down at his feet, happy to see him again.

"Latte?" Ben asked in mock cheerfulness from the kitchen.

"Sure. Thanks," the agent replied, head buried in the file.

Ben came back after a few minutes and set down the coffees.

"OK, man, where are we?"

"Same place, just getting a little riskier. South Africa isn't Europe, and the brass are starting to get squeamish. But we still have the go-ahead, so we are still going ahead. You still up for this?"

"Is my immunity agreement signed yet?"

"No. Sorry, dude."

"Then I am still up for this. What next?"

"You fly to San Francisco on Friday, meet with our target, and then on to Johannesburg with him. I'll be shadowing you the entire way, which is the good news."

"I'm starting to get tired of this good-news–bad-news thing."

"The bad news is that it's just me. I have some contacts with the South African national police, but we aren't sure how much we can trust them, so we can't let them in on everything. If it looks like it might be easy to swoop down on the deal and arrest everybody and get the money, we might bring them in, but at this point, everything is so dicey that the plan is that you just find the triggers and call me. I will grab them, and we can arrest your man back in San Francisco later… assuming ISIS doesn't whack him first."

Ben let the economy of that description sink in. He quickly put together all the factors and saw the outrageous risks and the fact that he was still hamstrung into this nightmare.

"Will you be tracking my cell phone while we are there?"

"Nope, couldn't get it authorized without notifying the locals, which we are going to try and avoid. You will have to update me constantly."

"So I am fully alone if I get made." It wasn't a question.

"I'll have the overwatch as close as I can without getting made myself. I understand you are in a tough position here, but I always believed that it's better to be judged by twelve than carried by six, so be careful, Ben."

"Careful. South Africa, ISIS, nuclear weapons. OK, Howie. I'll be careful," Ben said.

"Point taken. Sorry, man."

"Whatever."

He knew where he was, and he had looked at all the angles. This was what he had to work with: Special Agent Howard Goodman. They were married for the duration, no matter how it turned out.

"Enjoy the next couple of days, and gear up. As soon as you touch down in San Francisco, we are on, so keep your phone on and your eyes open. Remember, this is such a shit show that as soon as you spot the triggers, we are calling it. Easy. I will reach out to you in South Africa." He dropped an envelope containing the plane ticket to San Francisco on Ben's very worn coffee table and walked out the door. Ben leaned back onto his couch and rubbed the dog's head. He figured he could get two surf sessions in, maybe even a run, and still have enough time to get his gear together for the trip to Africa. He still needed clearance from Bob so Geronimo could come. He picked up his phone and texted Bob, asking for it.

"All good, let's RV in the morning and I will have it for you," said the response.

Ben went to the kitchen and pulled a Pacifico out of the fridge. He drifted into his garage and sat down in the driver's seat of his old jeep. Geronimo jumped into the passenger seat, just in case there was an adventure in the offing. Ben exhaled deeply and sat for a while, meditating on the operation. He knew that at some point soon, the adrenaline would take over, and he would actually start to enjoy it, that the riskier it got, the more he would want it; he would revert. On that note, Ben polished off his beer, left the empty bottle in the center console, and walked over to his toolbox. He pulled out his legally nonexistent Glock and a few magazines before returning to the kitchen. In his cupboard was a large can of incredibly cheap coffee. Ben didn't drink that shit; he had no idea how it got there—a previous tenant, perhaps? *Whatever.* He pulled out a large bowl and a very large plastic bag with a zipper closure and put both on the counter. He opened up the coffee and dumped it all into the bowl. He took the Glock and the magazines and made sure they were all loaded and in working order. Satisfied, he put them all in the plastic bag and zipped it shut. He put the bag into the empty coffee can and then dumped all the old coffee back inside, burying the gun. For the finale he taped ten one-hundred-dollar bills to the lid of the coffee can and then sealed it up. He took the can/gun back to the garage, where he pulled out a black duffel bag. He set the duffel bag on the ground and put the coffee can inside.

So it begins, he thought and went for another beer.

42

B ob knocked on Ben's door around dawn. Ben got up to answer it. Opening the door, the vet handed him a sheaf of papers.

"These should clear G-dog for your trip. You guys are good to go. Want to grab some waves right now? I am thinking of going down to The Cliffs."

Sunset Cliffs?

"Hell yes. Let me grab my stuff."

Ben grabbed the gear and an extra mammal and jumped into Bob's aging Toyota Land Cruiser. It was an understated vehicle for a guy who lived oceanfront in La Jolla, but perfect for the beach. They made their way down the coast; past Ocean Beach, one of the last holdouts of full-on hippie culture in California; and toward The Cliffs, pulling into the dirt lot at the end of the road. The remaining property southward belonged to the federal government. They would be going on foot from here. They changed into their suits and worked their way down the goat trail to the beach. Geronimo was in stray-dog heaven and took off. The two surfers walked a half mile to their spot. All along Sunset Cliffs, there were reef breaks every few hundred yards, each one slightly less crowded than the last. They arrived at their chosen break; nobody was out, and it looked good, three to five feet with no wind. They both paddled out and reached the lineup at virtually the same time. Without missing a beat, Ben turned and paddled for a big left-hander. He made the drop, flew down the glassy face in perfect California style, and kicked out, paddling back around the shoulder to his friend the drug dealer and animal doctor.

"What's the real deal behind your South Africa trip? You really going solo to surf and watch a pro contest? Doesn't sound like you," Bob said after taking a wave himself and paddling back.

"Truth?" Ben asked, not really giving a shit either way.

"Yeah, man. Of course. What is it?"

"Just an extension of the FBI fucking me over from beyond the grave. I can't or won't give you the details, but it is an undercover deal, and suffice it to say that I am not stoked," Ben replied, eyeing a bump on the horizon that he thought might have been the next set.

"Wow. That is a bummer, man," said the vet, taking it a bit too lightly, Ben thought, but then again, surfers on the whole were a pretty mellow group, so he let it go. He stroked out a few yards in anticipation of a larger wave.

"If you get in a jam down there, call me. I'm serious," Bob said, before taking a few strokes in the other direction then digging deep to catch a nice medium-size right.

They surfed together for another hour before a couple of other guys paddled out. This wasn't Ben and Bob's home break, so they didn't know them, but it was so far off the beaten path that nobody claimed any sort of rights here. The four just gave one another a quick nod and returned their gazes to the horizon. It was unspoken, but Ben figured they should call it a day. They had the place to themselves for over two hours—no need to be greedy. Ben caught one in most of the way and paddled in the rest of the way to the beach where Geronimo was digging a very large hole in the sand, looking for some unknown treasure. Ben posted up next to him and watched the surfers catch their waves. After a couple more, Bob paddled in as well. The three of them walked back to the truck in silence, fully sated. Back in Pacific Beach, Ben unloaded his board and wet suit onto the grass in his yard.

As Bob was getting back into his truck, he reiterated, "Seriously, bro, call me if you need anything. South Africa is pretty sketchy from what I remember."

With that he sped off. Ben was getting annoyed at the mama-bear routine but shook it off as he hosed down his board and suit with fresh water. He also tried to blast some of the sand off Geronimo, who dodged most of the spray. Ben then meticulously dried the board and brought it into his vault of a garage. He brought in the wetsuit as well, hanging it on a special hanger that wouldn't crease the shoulders.

He then set about the laborious process of packing for a trip to South Africa to participate in an undercover, black-market, nuclear-technology deal. He didn't really have a good list for that, but he reckoned he would just work in descending order of perceived importance to the trip. His pistol was already packed; next would be the surfboard. He was going to South Africa, after all, and it helped his cover. He pulled his big blue wave gun from the rack. This was the same board he had shaped for his sailing trip with Joe the year before, the same Joe who coincidentally bore complete responsibility for Ben's jacked-up, current predicament. This would not be easy to forgive Joe for, but it wasn't the surfboard's fault. It was good, and it was coming. Ben then chose an appropriate bag to protect the board from luggage handlers, customs officials, and the other dangers awaiting the fragile fiberglass surfcraft, then did some quick research on the water temps for this time of year in South Africa and selected a single wetsuit that would cover all options. A 4/3 O'Neill with a set of booties in case it got really cold. A few bars of wax, two extra leashes, and that section was complete. He took a break and went to the refrigerator. He reached for a Pacifico but stopped short. He closed the door and took a glass of water instead. He needed to focus. He sat down on his torn couch with his water. He wasn't sure how far down the paranoid rabbit hole he should go, but if his history was any indication, things could get weird very quickly, and it paid to be prepared. To that end, he started filling bags with freeze-dried food, a camp stove, a tent, a sleeping bag, anything he could think of that he might need to survive in Africa. He thought that if things went well, he might could just camp up and down the coast surfing after this thing was over. After the election, Ben wasn't feeling in a particular hurry to get back to the United States. By the time he was finished, he had enough gear to survive in Africa indefinitely. Whatever he didn't have he could buy when he got there.

The next day, he assembled all his gear on the sidewalk. On his way out of the door, almost as an afterthought, he grabbed his black diplomatic passport from his FBI days. It was long expired, but it was the only semiofficial form of identification he had and the only provable link that he wasn't some burned-out psycho working a black-market deal with ISIS. It was the one thing he had that would lend credence to his story if he had to tell it. He hailed a minivan and dragged his gear and one slightly perturbed dog down to Lindberg Field for his flight to San Francisco. He managed to get everyone and everything aboard with minimal headache and downed two cocktails on the short flight north. He hit the curb at SFO in the early afternoon and flagged a van to take his board, dog, and four bags of survival gear to the airport at Half Moon Bay, where Trentino's private jet was waiting to take them across the planet to Johannesburg. Ben knew Half Moon Bay from its surf reputation as home to Maverick's, the premier big-wave surfing spot on the mainland United States, not to mention one of the sharkiest. Ben had no interest. He and Geronimo rolled up to the flight line and started unloading. He was pretty low budget in most of his life, but he definitely appreciated the travel options of the one percenters. There were no security guards, no lines, no genital scanners, no hassles. Ben watched as the pilots walked around the plane looking for damage before taking off. Giancarlo came out of the slick-looking offices of the fixed base operator with a huge grin on his face.

"Amigos! I'm so glad that you guys came! It's good to see you. Leave all of your gear on the pavement; my man will load your things. I want to show you something," he gushed. His black eyes and scratched face from his climbing adventure had healed somewhat. Ben dropped his stuff and walked with him toward a large hangar with the door open, Geronimo trotting alongside. Inside was a large shipping container with the doors open. Ben could see two motorcycles, about a dozen tires, tools, and other racing detritus inside. He also noticed a few climbing ropes and other climbing gear.

The triggers are in here, Ben thought, looking around.

"Amazing, right? This whole container is getting flown out tomorrow and staged at the racetrack the day after we get to Jo'Burg. We live in truly amazing times, eh? You can throw your longboard in here, and it will be in South Africa with the rest of the stuff."

Ben couldn't tell if Trentino was on drugs or was just genuinely excited. Either way, Ben now had his search field narrowed significantly. If he could find the krytrons in this container when they got to the race, he could blow the whistle, call in the cavalry, and call it a day. He might actually get to surf after all.

"Let's get on the plane and get the hell out of here," Trentino said, trotting briskly in the direction of the jet. Ben dropped his surfboard and one of his bags by the container and walked in the direction of the jet with Geronimo following behind. In the bag was his coffee can/gun combo. He didn't like parting with it, but there was a decent chance that it would slip through with all the stuff in that container. Looking over his shoulder, Ben saw two hard-looking ex-military types loading his surfboard, his bag, then shutting the container and locking it. As they crossed the taxiway, a very attractive flight attendant was waiting by the gangway onto the Bombardier Global 6000. Ben and Giancarlo climbed the steps followed by a very enthusiastic mongrel street dog. Ben looked left into the cockpit where two pilots were going through their preflight check. The guy in the left seat looked familiar to him somehow. He had met so many people over the years, he may have seen him somewhere before; then again, maybe every middle-aged white guy was just starting to look the same to him. Ben noticed that his luggage was neatly stowed in the back and that a cocktail was waiting for him at his seat. There was also a bowl of water and a rawhide chew for Geronimo. It was looking to be a nice flight. He sat down, took a long drink on what he believed was an Old Fashioned, and buckled up. The younger pilot came out and introduced himself as Gary. He gave them a quick rundown on their flight and how they would need to stop for fuel in Cape Verde. The stop would provide enough time for everyone to get out of the plane, grab some food, and stretch their legs. The pilot then excused himself to the cockpit as the engines fired up, and they requested clearance to taxi out for takeoff. Ben pulled out a South African surf guide he had bought in Pacific Beach and started thumbing through it. He knew where he wanted to go, but he delighted in getting as much detail as possible about a place before he surfed it. Surfers are usually such a tight-lipped group that good data was hard to come by, so you had to take what you could get. He wanted to surf Jeffreys Bay. The town had one of the best right-handers on the planet, if you could get past the sharks. The guide's description of Supertubes didn't tell him anything he didn't already know. Namely that it was an amazing place to surf and was home to a famous pro-surfing contest where the year previously one of the contestants had got knocked off his board by a very large great white shark. Ben ignored that last part and started browsing through some of the other highlights of the South African surf scene. He stopped at a spot called Dungeons. He had heard of this place. The description read, "Dungeons sits on the Cape Peninsula outside of Hout Bay. One of the biggest surf spots in the world, it is a cold and forbidding stretch of water a mile offshore that faces directly into the roaring forties and the Great Southern Ocean. It is never short on swell. This giant wave breaks next to a seal colony in some of the sharkiest waters on Earth. Great Whites are common in the area. Experts or madmen only."

Ben drained his cocktail and leaned his head back. It was going to be a long flight, but he was almost looking forward to it. He could drink himself stupid, flirt with the flight attendant, and just hang out and enjoy the calm before what was likely to be a very big storm. Geronimo had a similar idea and curled up at the feet of the same flight attendant for takeoff. The twin jets roared as the throttles pitched forward, and they blasted up into open air and over the ocean. Airborne, they banked east and leveled off.

Once in level flight, the attendant stood up, gave Geronimo a pat, and walked back to where Ben and Giancarlo were sitting.

"My name is Katie, and I'll be with you for the duration. More drinks, gentlemen?" she asked.

"Yup," said Ben, holding his glass aloft.

"I'll go again as well," said the target.

"Dude, is this your plane?"

"Sort of. I just leased it for the trip. They say that if it floats, flies, or fucks, you are better off renting it," Giancarlo replied, smiling on one side of his mouth.

"Wow, fair enough. Did you grow up in San Francisco?" Ben asked, changing the subject as a deliberate attempt to build rapport, one of the skills he was trying to remember from his investigative days, before he had hung himself out on the ragged edge of society.

"Yeah, during the war, when he was very young, my dad was part of the Italian resistance. He ferried messages between the villages in Tuscany to the Allies. Supposedly he once killed an SS officer with his bare hands after he had discovered him sleeping in a barn. Anyway, Italy was so fucked up after the war, so he came over to California because it reminded him of Italy, and there was a pretty solid expat Italian community in the Bay Area. He had good technical skills, became an engineer, and then used his US Army contacts from the war to start selling to the government. I came along, grew up under his wing, and here we are," Trentino said without much enthusiasm. "What about you? What's your deal?" he asked, taking a huge ice cube into his mouth.

"You know the high points. I'm a lawyer, originally from Chicago. Came out west for school, fell in love with California and surfing, and never left. Simple," Ben said, strictly telling the truth but leaving out almost every relevant detail of his true life.

"Surfing, huh? I was always too scared of sharks, man. You have got to have pretty big ones to surf the Bay Area. I just stick to racing and climbing. Much safer."

Trentino waved at Katie for another drink, and she went to work.

"You feel like telling me about the FBI? Jail?" Trentino threw down as casually as possible.

Ben's blood ran cold. He was in a plane, over the ocean, fucked. He tried to remain calm. At the bureau, years ago, there had been a bulletin board above one of the copy machines. On it, someone had pinned a sheet of paper that said in handwritten scrawl:

ADMIT NOTHING.
DENY EVERYTHING.
MAKE COUNTER ACCUSATIONS.

He never knew who the author was nor the circumstances behind it being posted there, but if he was burned, it was going to be his mantra.

"I don't know what you are talking about," he said.

"C'mon, bro." Then, winking at the flight attendant, "Katie, will you get this guy another old fashioned to loosen his lips a bit?"

She mixed the drink and then came over and sat directly on Ben's lap, handed it to him, and whispered, "What is this about the FBI?"

Ben ignored her and looked straight at Trentino, thinking that he was about to start fighting for his life.

Ben assumed there was not likely to be any gunplay in an airplane, so he keyed up for an old-fashioned brawl.

"How much do you know?" Ben asked.

"Assume I know everything, and start at the beginning," Trentino oozed, clearly enjoying himself.

Denying everything wasn't going to work. Ben couldn't think of a good counter-accusation but he remembered that the best undercover agents used the truth as much as possible.

"I went FBI right out of law school, thought I could make a difference, liked it well enough. Accidentally killed a DEA agent who was trying to kill me. His brother was a DA with a hard-on for vengeance, and I went to the can for five years, came out, managed to keep my law license, and here I am on your jet," Ben said, scrutinizing Trentino's face for any indication that the game was up.

"I had one of my corporate security guys run you, and that's basically what they told me. I just wanted to see if you would cop to it. No big deal. Relax, man."

Ben breathed a little bit. "Not something I usually throw down in polite conversation, for obvious reasons."

"I get it, man. We all have secrets," Trentino said, holding his gaze and taking a long pull on his drink.

Ben excused himself to the bathroom. In the mirror he looked to himself like a madman, pale and sweaty, but he told himself it was all his imagination as he looked down at his shaking hands. He whizzed, splashed some water on his face, then remembered that as much as he was looking forward to returning to New Zealand, he was still an alcoholic nihilist. What did it matter if he got killed on this plane? Not much. The dog.

What would happen to the dog?

That was all it took to get his head back in the game. He was playing to stay out of jail, which meant a home and a life for his dog. Staying alive, while a practical necessity, was philosophically tertiary to those things. Satisfied that he had some sort of mental framework to use going forward, he left the tiny bathroom. Trentino was by now aggressively flirting with the flight attendant. So Ben mixed another drink and then went to the back of the plane to sleep. He took one sip and was out almost immediately. He dreamed of prison.

43

The rest of the long flight flashed past in a delirious set of images: Trentino throwing a ball down the aisle for Geronimo, Katie asleep with her mouth open, one of the pilots getting something from the bar, Katie preparing food for the passengers and crew. Ben spent most of this time sleeping or drinking, which put him in pretty rough shape when they landed in Johannesburg. He pulled himself together with some coffee at the private airport terminal, got his bags from the handler, and made his way through South African Immigration and Customs. Giancarlo had arranged a van to ferry them to their hotel in the supposedly trendy Melrose area of Johannesburg. As they traversed the city, Ben found it hard to imagine that such a place could exist in this city. Johannesburg had the feel of a place under siege. He had heard the crime statistics but was not ready for the visual assault of the towering walls, the concertina wire, and the alarming number of electric fences. Ben had once read that BMW made a car just for the South African market with flamethrowers that erupted from underneath as a deterrent for carjackers. Ben smirked at the thought of very staid German car engineers trying to figure out how to roast someone outside the vehicle while not killing its occupants; he left the historical implications alone. They rolled up to the African Pride Melrose Arch Hotel, and it did, in fact, look like they were in a cool area bustling with cafés and street life. When the hotel staff started to protest about Geronimo, Ben pulled out his wallet and started peeling off bills. He stopped peeling cash when the clerk stopped speaking, and all was forgiven. Giancarlo handed him a key.

"Get some sleep, dude. The container doesn't arrive until the day after tomorrow. Burn off your jet lag, and meet me for dinner tomorrow night here at the hotel. I have some business in town during the day, so you're on your own for a while. Get some sleep, hit the hotel gym, whatever. I'll catch you later."

Giancarlo veered down the hallway dragging his bags, looking very much the weary traveler. Ben did the same, taking all his gear and G-dog into the elevator. He ordered a burger from room service, cracked a beer from the minibar, and opened the e-mail app on his phone. In his inbox were several forwarded conspiracies from crazy Phil, one or two small legal solicitations from his weirdo friends in PB, and nothing from Jess. He closed it up and went to the window and stared out. The knock at the door brought him back to reality, and he let the hotel man into the room. Ben watched him carefully as he placed the room-service tray. He might have just been tired from the trip, but his paranoia was running full steam. The harder he scrutinized the hotel man, the more standoffish the guy got. By the end of the transaction, it was almost like a money drop for a hostage transfer. The burger safely in hand, Ben signed a big tip, feeling guilty, and the guy hauled ass out of there, clearly freaked out. He and Geronimo split the burger and fries then passed out on the giant fluffy bed.

Ben heard the crash of the cell door slamming shut, and he ripped awake, sweat soaking the bed. He squinted into the darkness and remembered where he was. Hotel room. Johannesburg. Not the segregation unit, Pelican Bay State Prison. But the noise? Had he actually heard something? Was someone in the room? He looked for Geronimo, who was laid out on the couch, head craned over at Ben as if to say, "What is wrong with you?"

Ben let it go—just another nighttime ghost paying him a visit.

44

The next morning, Ben got up and showered, absently feeling the scars from ghosts of bullets past. He was preparing to take a calculated risk. He was sure the triggers were in the shipping container; nothing big enough had been unloaded from the plane when they touched down. This meant he had a day to get ready. For what exactly, he wasn't sure, so he decided to overdo it a bit. He took Geronimo and left the hotel, hell-bent for coffee and possibly a bagel. He found both at a cart on the street, definitely not New York caliber but certainly good enough. He sat down at one of the outdoor tables and got to work on his phone. He quickly found the information he needed and started off. It was a two-mile walk, but after the flight and the drinking, he needed the exercise.

At the same time across town in Soweto, Giancarlo Trentino walked into the Golden Reef Casino. It was comparable to a modest casino in Las Vegas, which meant that it looked like an over-the-top gilded nightmare. He made his way to the central bar, which had a colonial English vibe, made with polished oak and backed by a large mirror showcasing the various alcohols. General Qureshi sat at the bar in a finely tailored black suit. With his white hair and dignified bearing, he could be almost any ethnicity. He certainly didn't look like one of Allah's warriors. Trentino hung back a moment to watch the old warrior. Qureshi was drinking water and visibly uncomfortable in such a palace of Western decadence. Trentino was happy to take the guy's money, but it still felt good to watch this asshole squirm a bit. He walked over, all smiles.

"Mohammed, *como estas?*" he asked, turning the screws with the Spanish.

"You know that I am not a Mexican, yes? That not all brown people are the same?" Mohammed growled.

"Just fucking with you, man. We still good to go?"

"Your money is here. I will deliver it at the handover of our electronics."

"Let's be clear: they are currently *my* electronics. They will become *your* electronics after we make the deal and after I get my money."

"Of course," Mohammed whispered, taking a drink of his water. "When and where?"

"On Sunday morning after the race. Bring a truck to Kruger National Park, go to the Roodewal Bush Lodge, and wait there. Do your best to pretend that you are on safari. Bring some binoculars, and work on your acting skills. I will bring the devices to you there no later than three p.m. Out in the bush, there will be nothing weird about a couple of guys talking on the side of the road. That part of the park is outside of cell phone coverage and is frequently patrolled by armed game wardens, so none of your fellow holy warriors can ambush me and vice versa. Sound good?"

"I am not a thief, but yes, your plan is acceptable. I will be there no later than noon." He drained his water and walked away.

Giancarlo watched him go, then ordered a scotch while turning to check out the ass of a passing waitress. He smiled at how well this seemed to be going.

At the same time, Ben was hitting his first errand of the day. He walked into the Johannesburg branch of Deutsche Bank. He had Geronimo decked out in his fake service vest, hoping to avoid any grief. Ben didn't think Johannesburg was the kind of place you could tie up a dog outside and hope to find him when you came back. He walked out several minutes later with €50,000; an equivalent amount of South African rand; and another 100 gold Krugerrands in case things really went to hell. He put it all in a very ratty-looking backpack. They walked east down the sidewalk toward errand number two. Within the hour, he pulled out of the dealership with a brand-new NGO, white Land Rover Defender 110, the travel mode of choice for well-heeled Africans. Geronimo hung his head out the window, reveling in the sounds and smells of Africa. Ben's last stop was to one of Johannesburg's many out-door/survival/hunting shops. By the time the day was over, his Land Rover was fitted with a rooftop tent, a refrigerator in the back, full vehicle-recovery gear, and everything else one would need to survive for an extended time in the bush. Ben had spent enough time in Baja with his jeep to guess what he needed. His system had more or less worked in the past, so he was sticking to it. The salesman was so excited about Ben's accumulation of adventure gear that he talked Ben into a pair of high-dollar but still civilian-grade night-vision goggles. Ben told himself he needed to buy them to maintain his cover, but truthfully, they just seemed like a cool toy.

Back in the car, he went over the equation in his mind. He was working with a black-market dealer in nuclear technologies, whom he was becoming friends with, and making a deal with the biggest terror group in the Middle East at the behest of the US government, who was blackmailing him and just might throw him in jail anyway. Yep, he may have been paranoid, but everyone was definitely out to get him. He drove the truck back to the hotel and parked it in the garage, satisfied that he had made some effort at an insurance policy if things went pear-shaped.

45

Mohammed had arrived in South Africa a week early to set up for the deal and minimize the risk that he would be double-crossed or killed. He was happy to pay for the triggers as planned, but despite his protestations to the contrary, he would be happy to steal them as well if he had to.

He had tracked the shipping container from the time it arrived in Durban to when it was delivered to the racetrack. He knew that a one-man surveillance operation was going to take its toll on him physically and psychologically, but in the end it would be worth the cost. The old warrior had at least one big battle left in him.

46

Ben and Giancarlo met in the lobby at 5:00 a.m. The setup was simple: there was a day of practice followed by qualifying, then the next day, the race. They planned to get there a bit early to open the container and get the bike ready. Ben got a coffee in the lobby while he waited for Giancarlo. When he finally showed, he seemed distracted. Whether this was his pre-race ritual or the stress of an illegal multimillion-dollar deal that might cause the end of the world, Ben couldn't tell. A black van pulled up outside, and they moved to get in, Trentino still not speaking. At the track they were ushered past the gate beneath a banner reading, "Welcome to the 2016 Kyalami Silverchief Challenge."

A track official pointed them to the pit area where the container was already staged. Trentino opened the container and switched on the lights. Inside was a mobile motorcycle garage. Clearly some money had been spent on its design. Ben hadn't noticed in San Francisco, but everything had a place, and each item was bolted or strapped down. Someone had even secured his old Baja surfboard in such a way to prevent damage during shipping. He spotted his bag tied to the side of the container. While Trentino was talking Ben casually walked over and picked it up. When he had first seen the container in San Francisco, he hadn't truly appreciated the build-out. This reminded him of his garage in Pacific Beach, and it appealed to his neuroses. He pulled back from his appreciation of the place and started scanning for what he wanted. Ben quickly looked over the interior for anything that looked like it could contain two hundred nuclear triggers. Everything looked like it was purpose-built for motorcycle racing, save for one pile in the corner. It looked to Ben like climbing gear: several dynamic ropes, harnesses, lots of anodized aluminum, and some black duffel bags. They had to be there. Trentino motioned for help getting the shiny BMW motorcycle out and onto the track, and together they muscled the machine into the sunlight. Ben thought he heard Trentino mumbling to himself, something about a mineshaft.

"Dude, what are you doing?" Ben asked.

"Just riding the course in my mind, man. Hard brakes, turn two, full throttle through the Mineshaft, et cetera."

"Mineshaft?"

"A nickname for a big drop on the track here. Supposed to be scary as hell, but we've been through the Corkscrew, right? We can handle it," he said quickly.

"We?"

"Yeah, man, we! I may be the one riding, but *we* are the team here, you and me! I can't do it without you. We win, right pal?"

"Fair enough, but be careful, man."

"Forget that; careful loses. I am here to win, and I need your help. FYI, it's open riding right now, so I need you to take a couple laps at fifty percent to tell me how the bike is working. Your helmet and leathers are in the container. I'm going to visualize the course for a few more minutes before getting out there myself. Just knock out a few laps, and don't crash, we only have one spare bike."

Ben walked into the container. He had to keep up appearances, so even though he had had no previous plans to ride, ride he would. He actually got a little excited about it. It would mean postponing his chance to look around the container for the triggers, but at the moment, all he could think about was getting on the bike and going really, really fast. He tried to ignore the fact that it was becoming obvious he and his target might have a lot more in common than he would like to admit. He grabbed his gear, suited up, and made his way out to the bike. Geronimo stayed back inside the cargo container and laid down on the pile of bags.

Good boy.

When Ben came out to their staging area, Giancarlo was sitting on the pavement in the lotus position with his eyes closed. Sensing Ben approaching, he silently pointed to the bike and then pointed to the track. Ben smirked and put on his helmet. He fired up the racing machine and felt the familiar rumble from Laguna Seca. From looking out on the track, it appeared to Ben that everyone already out there was taking it pretty easy. That belief was shattered as soon as he left the pit lane. The other riders were blasting past him within inches. It was nerve shattering. With every frightening pass, Ben felt the tires get warmer and his throttle hand get heavier. He knocked out two laps and started really hanging it out there on the third. He was doing his best to keep up with the traffic, and although the racers were probably not even breathing hard, Ben was doing everything he could to keep up, his world crystallized into shift, throttle, brake, knee out, turn, trail brake, throttle, straighten, upshift. He loved the focus. Getting lost in the deadly dance, he leaned way over going into turn twelve, knee on the pavement, the red-and-white stripes of the curbing flickering on the backs of his eyeballs as his vision tunneled. He was right at the limits of adhesion when his rear tire let go. He didn't panic and was able to save it with one or two big wobbles, but after he recovered, he called it a day. The bike worked fine, and he had a job to do. He pulled into the pits to see Giancarlo suited up and ready to go. His former Zen attitude replaced with ready tension.

"How did she work?" he asked with a clip.

Ben got off the bike. "All good, man. Have fun, and be safe."

"There is nothing safe about this, Ben. You know that."

The bike and rider pulled slowly down pit lane. Ben heard the throttle rip up as Giancarlo made his way onto the straight front wheel in the air, the high whine of the death machine hitting the redline followed by an immediate shift.

Ben wasn't sure how long Trentino would be out there on the track, so he wasn't going to poke around looking for the triggers too much during practice, maybe just a quick glance. He knew for a fact that in the afternoon he would have at least thirty minutes to himself when Trentino went out for qualifying laps. He would make his move then. If he could find them, he would call in the cavalry and call it a job well done. Ben immediately felt bad about it. His buddy routine with Trentino was working so well that it seemed to be cutting both ways. Ben shook off such thoughts and replaced them with those of survival, then wandered back to the shipping container and his job. He peered in and noticed that the pile of gear hadn't been obviously moved. His gig was almost over. He unfolded a camp chair, sat down in the pits, and cracked a bottle of water. Patience wasn't his strong suit after prison, but he channeled his younger self, the FBI man who could sit surveillance for hours, no problem. Geronimo lay on his back in the sun, tongue out to one side, dead asleep. Ben looked into the grandstands and among the scattered crowd saw someone with a set of binoculars staring straight back at him. He was sure he was under surveillance from Goodman, but somehow it didn't seem quite right; the attention seemed a bit too focused. Ben shrugged it off—nothing he could do about it. He told himself it was his overwatch and left it at that. He turned his thoughts to racing as he watched the bikes fly around the track.

47

General Mohammed Qureshi drank his mint tea as he sat in his truck and watched Ben Adams through a spotting scope from the hills outside the racetrack complex. He was a patient man.

48

Giancarlo Trentino came in from practice sweating but focused. Ben helped him put warmers on the tires while they topped off the fuel tank. Trentino took some water himself and caught his breath for a minute. They sat in silence for a few moments staring at the now quiet track. The loud-speaker announced that qualifying was about to begin and that all riders were to report to Start/Finish in five minutes. Ben and Trentino went to work. Ben pulled the tire warmers while Trentino put on his helmet and gloves then fired up the bike and motored his way down pit lane and out of sight. This was Ben's moment. He felt the adrenaline charge and his vision narrow as he went to make his move. He moved slowly; he knew he had more time than it seemed. This was a ten-min-ute job start to finish. Find the booty; make the call. He entered the container and switched on the lights, zeroed in on the pile of climbing gear, and made his way back. He got to the pile and started gingerly moving the ropes and cams to get at the duffel bags underneath. He used a very light touch. He smiled as he realized he was being stupid, that what he was looking for wasn't explosive nor radioactive, and he got more aggressive. Just as he reached the handle of one of the bags, he heard a voice from behind: "Excuse me?"

Ben jumped and almost fell down as he turned. He could see only the silhouette of a man with a clipboard backlit by the sunlight outside the container. The man walked forward as Ben straightened.

"Sorry to startle you. I am one of the racetrack stewards. I just came by to see if you guys need anything. I assume that you are the head mechanic?"

"Something like that," Ben replied, embarrassed for being so jumpy.

"Well, is everything satisfactory? We like to get any issues on the books as soon as possible so there aren't any surprises at the riders' meeting tomorrow. You know how it goes: one person speaks up, and then the meeting is two hours long, and we have to skip the race!" He guffawed loudly as he finished.

Ben faked a loud laugh himself, not sure if he sold it. "Yeah, I know. Everybody loves the sound of their own voice, but we're all good here for now. I'll check with my rider when he comes in, but we should be good to go. Where can I find you if we need anything?"

"Don't worry. I'll be around," the steward said, chipper as can be. He looked around the container, made a small tick on his clipboard, and turned and strode out.

Ben watched him leave, brought back to reality by a normal interaction.

What a nice guy, he thought. *Those South Africans sure are friendly and helpful…Fuck me. American accent.*

Ben reached down and picked up a large wrench and got ready to die. He worked his way down the side of the container, knowing he was inside a textbook example of the "fatal funnel." He would have to fight his way out. He slid down the right-hand side of the container with his back to the wall and the wrench cocked, and ready for the onslaught. He finally got to the end, still alive. He pulled a quick peek left and saw nothing, heard nothing. He stuck his head out a little farther and scanned around. Geronimo still lay on the pavement. The dog arched his eyebrows at him.

Ben put down the wrench and walked out into the sunlight as casually as he could and waited for the pain. It never came. He sat down in his folding chair and let his head roll back and closed his eyes.

Fuck.

49

Trentino had qualified fifth for the next day's race. It was a good showing. They locked the bike and other racing detritus in the container and piled into the van for the ride back to the hotel. Trentino was silent. He looked to be in the zone, mentally preparing to really hang it out there the next day. This was fine with Ben. It allowed him to keep his mental distance and avoid the uncomfortable questions that nag any good undercover operative. Namely that to be any good, you must empathize with your target, and in fact, you may come to actually like the people you will help throw into a cage. They got to their hotel and went up to their respective rooms, Geronimo right behind Ben. Ben had mentioned something about a possible dinner later, but Trentino blew him off. Ben went up to his room with his bag from the container. Once in the room, Ben dug into his bag for the coffee can. He opened it and immediately noticed that the money was gone. Digging deeper, he found that the gun and magazines were still there. He had what he needed. He took out the pistol, made sure it was still clean and oiled, and pulled a holster for it from the rest of his gear. Ben took a shower, then, not knowing what else to do, decided to stake out the well-appointed lobby of the hotel. Not only was there a bar down there, but Ben could spot Trentino leaving on the off chance the deal was going to go down tonight. He put the gun on his ankle, left Geronimo in the room watching HBO and headed downstairs.

Once in the lobby, he posted up on a corner stool at the bar that had good visibility of anyone coming or going. The cute female bartender rolled up, and he ordered a draft beer and a giant steak. She took his order and turned away. Ben felt like maybe she held his gaze a little longer than was strictly professional under the circumstances. He scanned the lobby. His read on the situation was that Trentino was genuinely interested in winning the race tomorrow and that most likely he was upstairs at the moment asleep, and his stakeout was good practice but probably not necessary. Not exactly Sherlock Holmes, but Ben was satisfied with his analysis. He was into his second beer when his steak arrived. The thing was ridiculously big and juicy looking. Africans seemed to take some serious pride in their braai. Ben was well into his third eye-rolling bite when he noticed the man. The American "race official" was strolling with purpose just past the bored-looking businessmen on the lobby couches. He was carrying a large black Pelican case, the type Ben was very familiar with. He noticed now that he had that build and walk like all the Spec Ops guys Ben used to know. This seemed bad. Ben threw a wad of rand on the bar and, pointing to his steak, said, "Save this for me," before moving off.

He stayed on the guy's six, giving him plenty of room until he got to the elevator bank. Ben hid behind a large potted plant, looking ridiculous as the American got on one of the elevators. As soon as the doors shut, Ben jogged over and watched the lighted floor indicators, willing them to stop. They stopped on five.

Five floors. Shit.

Ben blasted open the doors to the stairwell and climbed three at a time all the way to the fifth floor. He stopped on the landing and placed his palm on the door. He was panting hard. He cleared his mind and focused only on his breathing. He meditated in the exact same way he did trying to get through solitary confinement at Pelican Bay. Within a few moments, his breathing was almost at resting rate. He gently opened the door and looked out onto the floor. He saw the American walking away from him down the hallway. At the end of the corridor, he hooked a left. Ben jogged down the carpeted pathway as quietly as he could to the corner and gave a quick peek around to the other side. The American was three doors down and looked up right as Ben peeked around. Ben pulled his head back.

Damn.

The guy must not have spotted him because Ben heard the door open and shut. Ben was now stuck. He didn't really know how to proceed. He thought about just straight up knocking on the door and asking the guy, "What the fuck?" But that seemed a little reckless, even for Ben. Before he could make a plan, he heard the door open again. Ben hightailed it back to the stairwell, head back and arms pumping. He snuck in and quietly shut the door just as the American came around the corner. Ben decided that if the American decided to take the stairs this time, he was just going to haul off and punch him in the breadbasket and see what happened after that. Not great strategic thinking, to be sure. He breathed a small sigh of relief as he heard the elevator chime its arrival.

Ben heard a noise at the other end of the hallway. He spotted the source and quickly came up with a plan. He rapidly stripped down naked and stuffed his clothing and shoes into the icemaker, then quickly jogged over to the American's room. The ancient African housekeeper wheeled her trolley down the hallway until she spotted Ben—a stark-naked white man, his back to the door, one hand on his junk and the other in the air as if swearing to be the naked, the whole naked, and nothing but the naked, so help him God. The old woman cast her glance downward while shaking her head and fumbling for her keys. Without a word, she moved Ben aside and opened the door. Ben placed his palms together in thanks and slid into the room, noticing and smirking that the woman stole a glance at his crank before wheeling away. Ben went to work. He scanned the room and determined that he was alone. He started to search in earnest. It was over pretty quickly. The room was bare, as if nobody were staying in it. The bed hadn't been slept in. There was no clothing in the closet, no toiletries in the bathroom, and there was no luggage save for the single black Pelican case. Ben threw it open on the bed. Empty. There was no clue as to what it had once contained except that it was lined with foam, like you would use to transport high-end camera gear or a sniper's rifle. Not exactly a treasure trove of information. He walked over to a desk and took a roll of adhesive tape from the drawer. He carefully applied the tape to the case's handle and pulled back to reveal a few fingerprints. That he was the last person to handle the case and that he had no means of running prints wasn't lost on him, but it was his single investigatory avenue, so he went down it. He was naked and running out of time, so he got his extremely lame evidence and stuck his head out into the hallway. Looking left, then right, he sprinted to the icemaker, retrieved his gear in a bundle, and bolted to the relative safety of the stairwell. He emerged in the lobby, fully clothed, to his steak, pleased with himself for at least not getting caught.

Ben woke up early for the race. He tiptoed around the room so as not to wake the naked bartender from the lobby bar sleeping in his bed. She hadn't even mentioned the gun that now sat on the nightstand. He dressed and slipped out the door, Geronimo on his heels, clearly anxious to flee the room the first chance he got. He texted Trentino that he would meet him at the race so he would have his Land Rover after he wrapped this thing up. Ben walked down to the parking garage thinking that some South African surf exploration might be just the thing for him and G-dog after this adventure. There was rumored to be a good swell starting to fill in at JeffreysBaai tonight.

50

He crept through the early-morning light of Johannesburg in his Land Rover. Geronimo hung his head out of the window as usual, up for anything. He rolled up to the track, where the guards let him in after checking his name off the list. There was an electricity in the air as the race teams started their preparations. Everybody moving with focus. Everyone had a job, and everyone wanted to win. The crowd started to fill in around the pits with journalists, mechanics, and hangers on. The stadium started to fill. The life-and-death thrills of the race were already weighing on the atmosphere. Ben parked next to the container and noticed the doors were open. He jumped out of his car and swung around to look into the darkness of the container.

"Hey, bud! Give me a hand with this tire, would ya?" Trentino's voice shouted out of the darkness.

Ben walked in wordlessly and rolled the tire out of the way, his advantage gone. He peered into the corner and saw that the bags appeared undisturbed. Trentino beating him to the track this morning notwithstanding, things were going well. It would all be over soon, and he would be camping on the beach and surfing his head off.

"You are here early," Ben said.

"I can never sleep before a race, so I thought I would get a jump on organizing everything."

Trentino wheeled his motorcycle out of the container. Ben went to the back of the bike and helped him push it outside. They parked it on its stand and stood back to admire it, the morning sunlight reflected in the bodywork. Someone had been polishing. Trentino sat down to meditate as the loudspeaker announced the riders' meeting in ten minutes. Ben and Geronimo went off in search of coffee. Ben could see some of his minders in the stands already, and he felt comforted that this whole thing was almost over. He found the coffee table and poured a cup of the viscous liquid, adding in some bleached sugar and something powdered that made the coffee a lighter color but had seemingly no impact on taste. He put a stale bagel in his mouth and gave one to Geronimo, who trotted along next to him, bagel in mouth as well. They were an odd pair. Ben went back into the trailer and resisted the urge to start rifling around. He grabbed a chair, sat back, and waited. Geronimo sat down with a grunt and started working on his breakfast. After about thirty minutes, Trentino returned to the pit, fully dressed and helmeted. He sat down on the bike without a word and fired it up. The loudspeaker announced all racers to the start/finish line in five minutes. Ben squinted and saw that Trentino's eyes were closed but moving; he was riding the track in his mind. After a few moments, he opened his eyes, nodded to Ben, and said, "Good luck, dude," then rode off.

Good luck?

Ben tamped it all down for the moment and waited. By now the stands had started to fill up, and Ben could no longer spot whoever had been skylined and was watching him. He heard the announcer count down. At one, the roar of the bikes filled the air, and Ben felt a sympathetic jolt of adrenaline as the riders tore off hell-bent for leather. He took one single breath as a spectator of the race, then went to work. He walked straight to the back of the shipping container and to the corner with the climbing gear. He tossed aside the dirty ropes, cams, and gross shoes, and he got to the unmarked duffel bags. He pulled one out and unzipped it. It was filled filled with dirty and chalk covered climbing gear. The second bag revealed more of the same. The third bag was lighter when he grabbed it. He slowly unzipped it. There they were, as advertised; it was a big pile of nondescript electronics in foil wrapping. They looked innocuous, like they were bound for a dentist's office. Ben pulled out his phone and texted Goodman: "I have them. In the container at the racetrack. Come now."

Ben grabbed his surfboard off the wall, lashed it to the roof of the Land Rover, then walked to the door of the container and waited for the cavalry to arrive. He sipped his now cold coffee and watched the race go by. He knew each of those riders was living a lifetime on every lap, victories for passes executed, failures for not enough brake in a turn, costing half a second, watching the next rider pull away. A crest and ebb of emotions all within moments. It was a familiar feeling. Then he heard the impact. The smoke followed quickly, billowing skyward, pointing down to the accident. The crash was on the other side of the track, so he couldn't see it. The yellow flag went out, and the ambulance raced off. The announcer called the crash. The factory Honda rider had high sided and a privateer on a Ducati slammed straight into him. No word on their medical conditions yet. Even in motorcycle racing, there was no free lunch. Just like everything else, you want the thrills, you take the risks. Trentino rolled by with a group of riders under the caution flag and shot Ben a thumbs-up as he went by. Ben silently wished the downed riders good health and Giancarlo Godspeed and returned to his task. The end was in sight, and he was feeling good. After a few moments, a rental car rolled up, and out stepped Homeland Security special agent Howie Goodman, alone. He smiled broadly as he approached Ben.

"Well done, lad," he said, clapping him on the shoulder.

"Inside." Ben motioned toward the container.

Goodman walked in and let his eyes adjust to the light as Ben strolled past him to the bags. He pulled one and dropped it at Goodman's feet. They both crouched down to inspect their haul. Goodman pulled one of the krytrons out and examined it, then turned to face Ben and said, "Goofgurlgesprout."

"What?"

"*Harschcakstamportop!*" he screamed as blood ran out of his mouth and his arms fell limp. His eyes rolled back in his head, and he fell forward in a heap, his head slowly sliding off the large blade that had entered at the rear of his skull. The blade was attached to a man dressed in all black and was drawing back to give Ben a dose of the same as Geronimo lunged from behind and dug his teeth deep into the assassin's calf. Their assailant turned his attention to the dog. Already crouched, Ben pulled his 9 mm from his ankle and put one right in the chest. His opponent dropped his knife and staggered backward, swatting at the dog like some sort of insect. Ben lowered his weapon and watched the sick, lurching dance. Ben's attacker looked wild-eyed around the container then, seemingly possessed, picked up a ratchet and beamed it right at Ben. It made a solid *thunk* as it drilled him in the forehead. It was still on. Ben staggered backward and tripped over the duffel bags. In a second his assailant was on top of him in a fury, his breath reeking of pickled cabbage and his chest wound dripping blood onto Ben. Geronimo was still in the fight and on the guy's back. There were now four hands on the gun. Ben was trying to get the gun turned around to the guy's face so he could pull the trigger, but the assassin's fingers were working like crazy as they fought for control. The attacker's thumb moved down the body of the gun and found the magazine release. The full mag dropped onto Ben's chest.

Clever.

There was one left in the chamber. The guy's hands were like an octopus fighting for control of the gun. Ben was trying to simultaneously point it at his opponent's face and get his finger in the trigger guard to vaporize his head, but the guy was trying to do something else. Ben realized too late what was happening. The slide separated from the handle as the round ejected skyward and the gun fell to pieces on his chest. Ben started taking punches to the face repeatedly as he tried to come up with a new plan. As he flailed around, his right hand felt something on the ground that was metal and pointy; it was a sprocket for the BMW. He grabbed it and drove it straight into the temple of his nemesis. It was buried about an inch deep into the guy's temple, sticking out sideways like some sort of insane hat. The assassin froze and with a giant belch fell limp on top of Ben Adams. He rolled the carcass off him and jumped to his feet, ready for the next thing. He slowly caught his breath and realized that another attack wasn't immediately coming. He went over to Goodman and checked for a pulse. Nothing. Ben sighed and fished two five-rand coins out of his pocket and put them on Goodman's eyes for the ferryman. He walked over to the door of the container and peeked out as he listened to the sound of 10,000 rpm engines fly by. He closed the door and turned on the lights. Geronimo peed on the dead assassin, and Ben further assessed him. Asian man dressed in all black, midforties. He recognized him from Laguna Seca. Ben wasn't the only one playing the long game here for the triggers—not a huge surprise. He went through the dead man's pockets. They were virtually empty save for a hotel-room key and a photo of Ben Adams. Ben recognized that it was him, but it was another him. He couldn't pinpoint the exact day, but he knew the rest. It was taken outside the FBI building in San Diego, probably fifteen years ago and probably from a long-angle lens. Ben was wearing his FBI standard black suit, gun and badge on his hip, coffee in hand. Korean characters covered the margins and the lower half of the photo. Minus the coffee, it could have been someone else as far as Ben was concerned, but what this meant was that this guy worked for one of the Korean governments. Ben assumed the North, but at this point anything was possible. They were the type of people to build files on street-level FBI agents as a matter of course.

Ben thought for a second. His only real link to his deal with the US government lay dead at his feet. Ben knew nobody at HSI, and the people he knew at the FBI all hated him, save for Joe. He had to run. He quickly took photos of the entire scene with his telephone and went through Goodman's pockets, taking his credentials, phone, and knife. He put his gun back together, charged it, and holstered it, then picked up both of the duffel bags of triggers and quickly loaded them in the Rover. Geronimo jumped in, and they boned the fuck out of there at full throttle.

51

ohammed had been watching the container from his perch for days and was having a hard time focusing. Soon he nodded off. He awoke as the two Americans opened the door to the container and went in. Mohammed was nervous: he didn't really know who the players were. Were they Trentino's bagmen? Were they both about to get ripped off by someone else? High-dollar black-market deals were fraught with risk. He missed the order of the Iraqi Army. His fears grew as he watched the Korean assassin follow the Americans in a few moments later. He waited. It seemed like an eternity before the dark-haired American stumbled out of the container covered in blood and with his terrible-looking dog. He appeared disheveled and panicked, and he carried a duffel bag, which had to be his cargo. The American jogged over to a white Land Rover, tossed in the bag, held the door for the dog, and burned out of there fast. Mohammed wasn't sure how this was all going to play out, but the future of the caliphate depended on it. He had to stay with his triggers. He worked very hard to restrain himself as he turned the ignition in his Toyota Hilux and eased out of the dirt parking lot he was in, on an intercept course with the route of the Land Rover. He couldn't lose him.

52

Ben trucked north toward Botswana. His normal paranoia was serving him well at the moment. He had checked out of the hotel that morning, and everything he had was in the fully fueled safari rig. Ben didn't know that much about Africa, but he assumed that even the mighty US government couldn't get word to remote African border crossings before he got to one and was across. His only plan was to disappear into the bush for a bit until he could get a handle on the situation. He had read once that when asked how he was so successful, the Red Baron said it was because he would run as often as he would fight. In any situation, if the odds weren't completely favorable to him, he would flee and thus live to fight another day. Ben thought this was terrific advice at the moment. He had multiple enemies and no friends besides Geronimo; the odds were definitely not favorable.

On the highway outside of Jo'burg headed north, Ben pulled off on the dirt shoulder and pulled out a map. He unfolded it on the hood as he looked for his crossing. He noticed the silver Toyota Hilux pass him and turn off into the desert a few hundred yards ahead. It didn't register as an overt threat. On his map Ben found a crossing into Botswana named Martins Drift, about halfway to Zimbabwe. It didn't even seem to have much of a village associated with it as far as Ben could tell. It would have to do. Satisfied that the crossing was his best chance at getting out of the country undetected, he jumped back in the car and continued north.

After a few hours, Ben approached the border crossing by driving over the old bridge spanning the Limpopo River. It was just a collection of cinder-block buildings in government style familiar around the world, connecting two sides of a two-lane, crumbling highway. He slowed down as he approached, knowing full well it was silly: there wouldn't be a platoon of soldiers there to kill him. He would simply be told to "wait just a moment" while the border control officer went into a back room; then several minutes later, some other officers would come in from the outside and sack him up. He would have little notice and virtually no time to escape. He just had to risk it. He parked the car, eyes alert for anything unusual. It all seemed good, but since he had never been here before, he really had no idea. A baboon jumped on the hood and started screaming at Geronimo through the windshield. Ben hit the windshield washers and the primate bolted. Ben went into the office and got in line. There were three people ahead of him. The moments dragged on. Every time he heard a phone ring, he wondered if that was the call that was going to end his trip. By the time he got to the counter, he was sweating furiously. He had thought he was tougher than this, but then the thought of a dead HSI agent's creds and two hundred nuclear triggers in his car added some validity to his anxiety. The immigration officer was helpful and cheerful, thanking him for visiting South Africa and sending him on his way. One down. The car had to go through outbound South African Customs. He was waved through after a perfunctory look in the windows. Two down. He eased a little. He still had to get through Immigration and Customs in Botswana, but if they hadn't got to the South African officials yet, Botswana was even less likely. He breezed through both and hit the road north. He let go with a huge exhale. He had no medium- or long-term plan, but he was OK for the moment, he had money and mobility.

Not really knowing where he was going, Ben just kept driving. He blasted his horn along the way to reroute the many warthogs trying to kill themselves by bolting from the brush and flinging themselves under the wheels of his Land Rover. The scenery flashing by the window was almost cliché: giraffes standing tall above the acacias as they watched the traffic, the occasional elephant, and the not-so-occasional piles of elephant poop in the road that exploded in a satisfying way every time they were hit with the car. After a few hours, Ben seemed to relax a little bit, in tandem with the sun going down. Ben felt hidden in the darkness. A small part of Ben's mind reminded him that nighttime Africa had its own host of dangers, but compared to the international all-star hit team that seemed to be after him, getting eaten by a lion while he slept sounded downright relaxing. Ben planned on just pulling over into the bush and flipping open the roof tent and going to sleep, but as he slowed down along the shoulder to look for a track leading away from the pavement, he came upon some sort of camp in the middle of the savannah. It was called the "Last Chance Bush Camp," and it was surrounded by a large *boma*, which is a large natural fence created out of the thorny brush to keep out the wildlife.

Ben pulled into the fort and found what looked like a postapocalyptic RV park. It was an organized campground centered around a thatched-roof bar. The park was sparsely filled with various overland rigs, some with European plates, suggesting a very long trip south. Some were rentals, and some were privately owned with South African or Botswanan plates like Ben's. Ben picked a spot on the edge of the park and closer to the boma, sticking with his belief that he had much more to fear from men than from animals at this point. He and Geronimo jumped out of the car and wandered into the bar to pay for their stay. They were inside the bar when the gray Toyota cruised in past the gate. Inside the bar was a very motley crew of Afrikaners, other white Africans, and a scattering of San Bushmen who were playing pool. One toothless guy who had clearly had at least eleven Tusker beers thought it was hilarious when his own dog (some sort of sheepdog to Ben's eye) would mercilessly hump his leg. The guy would laugh like crazy until he shook the dog loose. Geronimo looked up at Ben for an explanation. Ben shrugged his shoulders and sat down at the bar. He ordered a beer and told the barman which site he had parked in. The barman took his money for the night and the beer and went back to chatting with the rotund truck driver at the other end of the bar. The guy apparently had just delivered the beers they were drinking and was the local hero at the moment as the town had been out of beer for some time. Ben took another to go and walked back to his truck.

It could have been the beer, but Ben was starting to relax. He thought back to Goodman. He was so freaked out in his escape, he had almost forgotten about the hardworking federal agent whose body was probably still cooling off. He had liked Goodman well enough, and he felt bad, but that was the job. Ben was alive. Goodman wasn't. It wasn't justice; it just was. He flashed through the events of the last few days, not exactly satisfied, but he had prepared, and he had escaped. He had no idea what his long-term prospects were, but he had the booty. He pondered his situation. He felt reasonably safe in a separate country from where the murders had taken place. He thought maybe, just maybe, that everything could work out OK. Either way, he had a nice campsite, his dog, and a beer in Africa. If the world ended tomorrow, at least tonight was pretty good. Ben folded out his tent, got a fire going, and rummaged around his icebox for dinner. Choosing a handful of *boerewors* he had bought in Johannesburg, he put them on sticks and set them to roast in the fire. Ben and the dog sat around the fire munching the exotic sausages, letting the adrenaline fade away. Ben ambled back to the bar for a few more beers then returned to his place at the fire. Sated and drunk, Ben lifted Geronimo up into the tent and crawled in behind him and promptly fell asleep.

The screaming woke him up. He quickly shook out his head and was on the ground in seconds, pistol out. His blood was up; it sounded like a serious fight was going on somewhere in the camp. Barefoot and shirtless, Ben, with Geronimo in tow, made his way toward the sounds, moving from cover to cover. He found the source of the fight. It seemed to be coming from inside the rooftop tent of one of the other safari vehicles. It was part of a group of vehicles surrounding a dwindling campfire. Whatever was happening in that tent was clearly bad: the yelling and the banging echoed through the night. Ben sat, ready to act, but unclear as to what was happening, he held back in the shadows.

One of the other tents zipped open, and Ben swung his pistol toward it. Over the tops of the sights, he saw a clearly inebriated man try to get out onto the ladder. He missed his footing entirely and fell seven feet flat onto his back in a cloud of dust. Ben cracked off a short laugh and refocused his attention on the murder going on in the next vehicle. As the guy on the ground staggered to his feet, the screaming and the violence stopped as suddenly as it had started. There was now low murmuring coming from the tent. After a few minutes, the tent unzipped, and a very disheveled-looking couple stuck both of their heads out.

"Sorry, everyone," the woman said in an American accent. "Brandon was just having a nightmare. I think the malarial meds are messing with his brain. Everyone is OK. Please go back to sleep."

They both sheepishly retracted into the tent and zipped it closed. The dust-covered skydiver shook it off and climbed slowly back into his perch. Ben had skipped the malarial drugs for this reason. He was hanging on by such a thin thread as it was that he didn't need any additional night terrors. Ben lowered his weapon and walked barefoot through the dust back to his tent rattled by the adrenaline.

53

Mohammed was now certain that this wasn't part of the plan and that Trentino would never make their rendezvous at Kruger. Something had gone seriously wrong, and this American was the reason. As much as Mohammed had been planning for a straight-across exchange, this new development meant he had a shot at getting the triggers and keeping the money. The bad news was that he was now going to have to take them by force, and he was alone. No matter, the old warrior had been in fights much worse than this. He wasn't under any real pressure; he would just follow his target, and when the opportunity arose, he would retrieve his items.

Ben woke up feeling a little better. Last night's events had lightened his mood a bit. He got his fire going and prepped his French press. Some coffee and some reheated boerewors and he was satisfied. He broke down his camp and rolled out. He still didn't have a destination; he just plunged deeper into the Kalahari. Driving helped him think. His main contact on this operation was dead. He had killed some sort of spook; *Who can I trust? Lanahan.* That was his only move: call Joe Lanahan in Puerto Vallarta, explain the situation, and trade the triggers for his immunity and safe passage. It was Joe's stupid fault that he had got roped into this in the first place. Ben pulled off the paved road and into the bush. He parked and made sure his truck couldn't easily be seen from the highway. He was going to whiz then use the sat phone Bob had given him to make the call. Satisfied that he had some sort of plan, he took care of his business on an acacia, and Geronimo followed suit. Finished, he dialed his old friend at the FBI. He heard the buzzes and clicks as the phone linked up to space and then around the world, presumably to a very nice Beneteau sailboat moored in Banderas Bay.

"Hello."

"Joe, it's Ben."

"Where the fuck are you, dude?"

"I don't know. Kalahari somewhere."

"What happened? Goodman is dead. So is some kind of North Korean superspy, and the triggers are missing."

"I have the triggers."

"Thank fucking God. I might get to keep my job, and you might not go to jail."

"I still want immunity, Joe."

"I am sure I can work that out. Just get your ass and those triggers to the embassy in Johannesburg as fast as you can, and I will work from here on your situation."

"Roger that."

Ben clicked off. He wasn't just going to roll into the embassy willy-nilly, but he would get back to Jo'burg and then get confirmation from Joe that all was well before he made any moves. Ultimately, he would have to take him at his word, and although not ideal, it was probably good enough given the options. Ben went to his cooler at the back of his rig and started rummaging around for a bottle of water when he felt the gun barrel on his neck. He froze and looked sideways at the wizened figure next to him.

Where the fuck did this guy come from?

"Slowly, my friend, very slowly," the man with the gun whispered.

Ben pulled his hands out of the cooler and slowly turned to face him.

"Where are they?"

"Back seat."

The Iraqi went to the back door and opened it. The dog leaped out in full attack mode. Qureshi was surprised but still reacted. He quickly got the gun up and shot. The dog cried out in pain and cartwheeled into the scrub, trailing blood with the general firing after him. Ben lunged with everything he had. Mohammed quickly turned toward him, and the world went black.

Ben could feel the pain before he opened his eyes. He thought about his dog. Surely dead or dying. He moved his face around and felt the dried blood crack and fall away from his cheek. He opened his left eye, his right stubbornly remaining closed. He was in a vehicle. He was in the driver's seat. His hands were duct-taped to the steering wheel. He looked left to see Mohammed in the passenger seat, a pistol in his left hand pointed at Ben's abdomen. It wasn't clear to Ben why he was still alive until he saw a busload of tourists on safari drive by on the road.

"OK, let's go," said the Iraqi, reaching over to start the truck and put it in gear.

The Muzak version of "The Girl From Ipanema" softly played through the car stereo. Ben did as he was told and accelerated the truck onto the road. He caught a glimpse of his Land Rover with the telltale blue surfboard on the roof in the rearview mirror as he pulled out, partially hidden by branches. He had some idea of where he was. With the pounding in his head, Ben didn't care if ISIS reduced itself and the rest of humanity to radioactive ash. Politics and war could get stuffed, but if it was the last thing he ever did, he was going to kill the man next to him.

54

They drove for about an hour on the blacktop. Ben marked off about forty-five miles on the odometer, trying to maintain some semblance of location in case he could get a call out and/or get away. Mohammed motioned for him to leave the road onto a sandy two-track leading into the grassland. Ben made another mental note of the mileage. They drove and drove, snaking through the African savannah. Ben constantly looking for another vehicle or some way out. There was nothing. They drove for an hour, just over thirty miles. Ben pulled over next to a huge baobab tree. He felt a drop of something running down his face; he couldn't tell if it was sweat or blood. He was only rage. Ben knew that when you plan for revenge, it is best to first dig two graves, but he didn't care. He had pretty much had the first one dug long ago; Mohammed's would just be a bonus. Mohammed flicked out a knife and carefully, keeping the gun on his man, cut Ben's hands away from the steering wheel and motioned for him to get out. There was only one reason to come out here. Ben knew that this was it and that the only reason he wasn't dead already was because his captor didn't want to drive home sitting on a blood-soaked car seat. Ben looked into the distance at some low volcanic mountains rising up from the desert floor. Nobody would hear the shot. He closed his eyes, tilted his head back, and took a deep breath of the clean desert air. He felt the barrel prod him away from the vehicle.

"Kneel, please," Qureshi said courteously.

Ben did as he was told.

"You are free to pray now," Qureshi said, inching closer to the kneeling man.

Ben closed his eyes, letting all his senses speak to him. He listened to the crunching of the steps behind him. When he felt like Mohammed was as close as he was going to get before shooting, he dropped down to all fours and donkey kicked him hard, right in the testicles. It was an absurd-looking move but a direct hit that sent the warrior reeling. Ben jumped to his feet and came at him hard. Mohammed got one shot off, grazing Ben's head. He flinched but kept coming. Ben got both hands on the pistol, rotated it quickly toward his adversary's center, and yanked hard with his whole body the way he was taught all those years ago. It fucking worked: the gun ripped out of Mohammed's hands, and Ben had it now. Ben raised the gun, aiming it straight at his enemy's head, and pulled the trigger. *Click.* Jammed. The fight was still on.

Before Ben could clear the jam, Mohammed drilled him hard in the face with his fist. Ben fell down on his back, and the warrior was on him. Ben launched his hips straight up off the ground and flipped Qureshi up and over his head when the first bullet hit the ground next to him, sending up a plume of dust. He heard the shot a second later. *Sniper.* Ben and Mohammed both recognized the new threat and rolled away from each other through the dust to cover as two more shots hit the dirt between them. It wasn't clear who the target was. They could see each other from their respective shrubs. The pistol impotent in the dirt between them. Both men looked murder at each other. Ben for vengeance and Mohammed because he was Mohammed. Ben lunged from cover at his enemy, but another bullet in his path stopped him cold, and he retreated back to cover. Mohammed reacquainted himself with his priorities and bolted to the Toyota, a series of bullets following at his feet. He flung open the driver's door as a bullet pierced the front tire, quickly followed by two more to the radiator, which spilled its contents down the front bumper. Crouching, Mohammed reached into the back and grabbed the duffel bag full of the deadly technology as the rear tire of the truck took some shots for good measure. He did some quick triangulating and ran off into the distance with the triggers, using the truck for cover. Ben bolted after him and felt a sharp pain on the side of his head followed by the crack of the rifle. He dove into a shrub and felt his ear. His hand came back bloody but only just. He was barely nicked. A warning. Whoever it was, the sniper didn't want to kill Ben, but he didn't want him following the Iraqi either. Ben sat in the shrub contemplating his options. Dog gone. Triggers gone. Immunity almost certainly gone. Snake eyes. One option left: run for it. Probably for the rest of his life.

Thirty miles, more or less, vaguely south was his Land Rover. He was going to have to hoof it for thirty miles in Africa, in the middle of the day with no water. Ben didn't particularly like his odds, particularly with the large selection of predators roaming around, but this was what he was doing. He thought the paved road they had driven crossed Botswana more or less east to west and that they had turned into the bush going north. The track zigged and zagged through the savannah, so it was only a basic direction. Thirty miles. Overland. On foot. In Africa. At least the weather was nice, and the terrain looked mostly flat. He took a glance at the sun, guessed which way was south, and started walking.

He walked for miles; it felt like a good pace. He could do this. It seemed strange that an environment so dry could support so many large animals. Ben saw giraffes cruising through the brush, their heads like periscopes above the trees. He saw seemingly limitless herds of springboks and other ungulates that Ben didn't know what to call. Eland? Kudu? He had no idea. What he did know was that he was sharing the environment with the things that ate those big things. This was not comforting.

Ben had walked for a few hours, and the sun was making its way toward the horizon when he saw his first elephant. It might be more accurate to say it saw him. Ben was walking along a game path that split between several medium-size trees and bushes, and as soon as he got alongside them, a loud trumpet blast ripped into Ben's ear as a large female elephant reared and bolted away. The thing was three feet from him, and he hadn't seen or heard it until it was running away. This did not bode well for Ben's situational awareness in the wild. He was pretty sharp in the city, but out here he was just walking meat. He made his way into a clearing where he saw the rest of the elephant herd browsing on the vegetation. He sat on a fallen log to watch them. He took a page from their book and re-laxed for a moment. Some of the males kept a wary eye on Ben but seemed calm enough to keep enjoying their day.

For the first time, Ben noticed that his lips were get-ting dry and cracked. He could definitely use some wa-ter. He remembered the possibly bogus rule of threes for survival: that you could survive three minutes without air, three days without water, and three weeks without food. As hungry as he was getting, he doubted that last part.

He tried some amateur survival strategy and tried to eat what the elephants were eating, but they just plowed through thorny and bark-covered acacia trees without even flinching. Ben softened up and chewed through one acacia thorn and decided he probably preferred starvation and would just hope he could get to civilization before his three days without water were up. He was a little hungover and already dehydrated, so he thought he had better make it to a village by tomorrow afternoon to be sure. With the sun getting lower and Ben without a light, he decided he had better make some sort of camp. He figured his best chance of survival through the night would be to depend on a boma similar to the one around the campground, so he set to work. The elephants had left enough detritus from their feeding to give Ben plenty of raw materials to work with. He didn't want to burn his water sweating, but he figured it was probably better to die of thirst tomorrow than to be eaten tonight, so he kept at it. After a few hours, and just as the sun went down, he was finished. It didn't look so much like a boma as much as a giant pile of spiky plants, but Ben had created a small space within where he could sleep. It wasn't much, but he thought it might do the trick. He crawled inside with a large stick to poke at anything that came through the "door" and lay down in the dust, trying to moisten his lips with his parched tongue.

The night passed in a delirious haze. Ben had never tried LSD, nor had he had malaria, but he imagined that how he felt that night was how each of those things must feel. It was cold, not life-threateningly cold but enough for Ben to spend the entire night shivering. He kept waking up, hearing noises. *Footsteps? Friend? Yeah, right. Foe? Unknown.* He would try to fall back asleep after what seemed to be the proper amount of time of lying still and waiting to die, but then his thirst would keep him up. He started fantasizing about all things water. He dreamed of surfing in fresh water, where he could just scoop it up in his hands as he surfed and gulp as much as he wanted; then he would hear a noise, wake up, and the process would start over.

When dawn finally broke, Ben could tell he was at best 50 percent effective for whatever was coming his way today. The bruises from his recent battles were definitely still fresh. Still, he was glad to see the sun. Its warmth loosened up his stiff muscles, and it felt like the blood was flowing back into his limbs as he stretched and crawled out of his artisanal fort/prison. His stomach was definitely letting him know what time it was. He tried to ignore it, knowing that water was what he needed. He could not ignore his thirst. He looked at the sun and guessed its direction was vaguely east, trying with virtually no ability to discern how the sun's place on the horizon would be affected by the low latitudes of southern Africa. Coming to some sort of conclusion, he continued heading what he thought was south. Southern Africa is a pretty flat place, which makes for easy walking but difficult direction finding. Ben could see some mountains in the distance, toward the west. He did his best to keep the mountains on his right and track in a straight line toward what he hoped was the road. His route was zigzagging through the large acacias, baobabs, and other strange plant life of Africa, and Ben knew he was probably doubling the length of the trip having to navigate around all the obstacles, but if the sun ended up on his right at the end of the day, he would have moved southward, closer to his goal.

As the morning ran on, the temperature went up. Ben's thirst was bullying him. He was starting to have a difficult time swallowing, and every time he licked his dry and cracked lips, there was a little less moisture transferred. He kept walking. At around noon, Ben was having trouble distinguishing the real animals around him from the ones in his mind. He also started seeing and hearing signs of water. He would notice a cluster of trees in the distance and think they indicated a riverbank. When he got there, he realized they were just as evenly spaced as every other tree; they had just lined up a little bit more, giving Ben's desperate mind all it needed to think that there lay salvation. Occasionally there would be a breeze, and to Ben it sounded like Victoria Falls, which somehow seemed tantalizingly close, even though he knew it was at least 150 miles away. That dream would die as well when the breeze revealed itself for what it was.

Ben kept walking. Soon, he lost track of time; it seemed like it was afternoon. His mouth was now totally dry, and there was nothing to help his lips, which were now receding from his teeth. He had read somewhere that with extreme thirst the blood thickened up and became hard to circulate. That sounded about right. His mouth was now permanently open. His teeth were now leading the body, jaw hanging loose as his tongue hardened into jerky. Blinking, his eyes now hurt. Ben thought he saw a lion. *Real?* He hoped so. He liked animals; they would like him too. It was getting like that. Ben's footsteps grew more sluggish. His feet dragged on each one. At some point, Ben was in the dirt. He didn't know how it had happened, just that his face was now in the sand. He looked up to see two bony feet poking out from under a black robe. He followed the folds of the robe upward with his eyes. It was Death. Ben nodded, understanding, but thought he should say something.

"Can you spare me for another year? Could you wait to call me another day?" he whispered.

Death slowly shrugged. He then raised his arm and pointed his skeletal hand toward Ben's feet. Ben inched his shrunken head around. At his feet was his dog, Geronimo, vigorously biting his boot.

He wants to play. Good dog, he thought, reaching his hand out. He couldn't quite reach his furry friend and fell backward into the dirt. He looked skyward to see that Death was gone.

Gone for a smoothie, maybe. That's nice.

Geronimo was playing it a little rough on his boots. It seemed like he was almost dragging him around.

That crazy dog.

Ben closed his eyes, thinking a nap might be a good idea. G-dog was self-entertaining at the moment, so Ben really didn't have anything to do. As he closed his eyes and started to drift off, he saw Jessica's face. He smiled. She smiled. Then her face changed. She got angry. She leaned in really close to Ben's face and screamed, "*Waaaaake uuuup!*"

This is bullshit, Ben thought and shook his head. It was sleep time. She kept screaming at him.

What is wrong with her?

The yelling wouldn't stop. Ben finally gave in and sat up, opening his eyes. As his surroundings took shape through his scorched eyes, he realized he was being dragged by his feet into the bush by three cape hunting dogs, and he was the one screaming. He delivered a few quick kicks and they retreated for a moment. They started in again. Ben grabbed and threw a small rock. The dogs went and regrouped under the shade of large bush. They could wait.

Fuck them. They can wait forever, Ben thought, dragging himself to his feet. He tried to yell at them to scare them off but could get out only a dry hiss. He loped off into the bush, hoping to ditch his pursuers. The dogs knew the score and kept pace at a safe distance, waiting for him to drop. They weren't the only ones who knew what was up. Death was in the air, and several cape griffons landed and hopped along, hoping to get a piece of the human when the time came.

Ben had a new motivation: not to feed those animals. He would stay alive out of spite. In his delirium, he reasoned that if the dogs had just been a little nicer to him, he would have stayed down, but they were rude in their handling of him and should be denied any meal related to the carcass of Ben Adams.

That will teach them.

Ben had clearly gone around the bend but was still walking, still more or less south. As night fell, even Ben's dried-up and virtually useless brain could tell that the game was going to be up soon. His tongue was so dry and hardened that it was clicking against his teeth like a striker in a bell as he walked. Since he didn't have a better plan and was still angry about the dogs, he kept walking. The stars were out, and Ben thought they were beautiful. They didn't have skies like this in California. The stars were everywhere, floating around him. He was swimming through the universe. His atoms were being dispersed through the cosmos. Two stars grew nearer. They were getting so big that Ben could almost touch them. The stars started screeching. Ben covered his ears; he didn't know what was happening. The world was suddenly very bright, then totally dark.

55

en slowly became aware of the sound of wind. He was still so thirsty. He couldn't be sure his eyes had been closed, but the world started coming into focus. He was in a car. The car was moving. An old Mercedes, something like a Lebanese taxi. It was daylight. He looked to his right and saw boobs. He completed his intake of the situation. He was a passenger in a car, on a highway, driven by a stunning African woman in a filled-out tank top and jeans and a closely shaved head. It was hard to tell because she was sitting down, but she had to be six feet tall and as fit as anybody in the WNBA. She noticed Ben moving.

"I thought you were dead, man. Last night you crawled out into the road like a warthog. I almost ran you down," she said in an accent part English, part Dutch, and part Zulu.

"Where are we?" croaked out Ben.

"Goin' to Maun. There is a hospital there."

"No, please turn around. Must get my car. Hospital later."

She looked at him skeptically.

"There is money," he said.

"Money? How much money?"

"Five thousand euros. Just to get me back to my car. It is on the road to Martins Drift. It is a matter of life and death. Please," he said, staring straight ahead.

"OK, I'll take half now, half when I drop you off. I have business in Maun myself, and this is going to set me back," she said, arching her eyebrows.

"I can't give you half now. I have nothing. Look at me; you must know that. You have to trust me."

"I doan have to do nutteeng," she said, her accent getting thicker. "But I'll do it, and if you doan pay, I'll kill you myself."

That sounded fair enough to Ben. If his Land Rover wasn't there, he was certainly dead, anyway. She pulled off and made a U-turn. She got up to speed going the other direction and handed him a bottle of water.

"Thanks. Let me know when we are getting close. What is your name, by the way?"

"It is at least one hour, and you can call me Zak," she said.

"Zak?"

"Zak."

Ben closed his eyes and thought about the last few days, SA Goodman, the ninja, Mohammed, the sniper, and Geronimo. If he had had the moisture to spare, tears would have come. He hadn't realized he was capable of such sadness. Up to that point, Ben had largely figured he was beyond human emotion. His sorrow at the loss of his dog was a huge surprise. He quietly let his heart break as they traveled east. After about forty-five minutes, Ben realized they had to be getting close. The kilometer markers were counting down to digits that were familiar to Ben.

"Slow down. We are getting close. It is a white Land Rover. It will be hidden behind some trees on the right-hand side of the road."

"How am I supposed to see it if it is hidden?" his driver asked with incredulity.

Ben could tell she was having second thoughts about this adventure, and if he didn't find his rig pretty quickly, she was liable to dump him in the desert in virtually the same condition she had found him.

"By the way, what kind of safari tourist has five thousand euros just lying around in their car?"

"A very cautious one…There!" he said, pointing into the trees.

Zak pulled off and around to where the Land Rover was parked. The car was surrounded by hyenas, clearly trying to get at something underneath it.

"You leave your food out?" the driver asked.

"No idea," Ben replied, terrified at whatever was under the car.

Zak laid on the horn and rolled her car up to the Land Rover, and the hyenas scattered. Ben wearily got out of the car. He watched as his driver unfolded herself and stood up. His original take was right: she was tall, beautiful, and fit. Despite the fact that Ben was pretty sure his sexuality was going to be dead for quite some time due to injury and lack of moisture, she was difficult not to look at. Ben finally looked away and got down on his knees to look for the keys he had dropped when Mohammed blasted him in the head with the butt of his pistol. He quickly found the keys but also saw what the hyenas were after.

Underneath the car was a pile of bloody fur, but it was somehow still breathing. One weary eye opened through the matted, blood-caked fur and saw Ben. The pile managed to thump its tail twice against the ground. Ben recognized the spots of his dog through the dirty fur. He immediately wiggled under the car and embraced his friend. He crawled his way out from under and went quickly to work opening up the truck and getting a blanket. Going back underneath, he slowly wiggled Geronimo onto the blanket and, inch by inch, dragged him out. Gently cradling him, he got him up into the back of the truck. Ben wasn't in much better shape himself, but he wasn't feeling any pain at the moment, his happiness at finding his only friend eclipsing everything. He gave the dog some water, which, lying sideways, he tried and mostly failed to lap up. Ben took another drink himself and went to it. He started rinsing and cutting away hair and found the bullet wound. Looked like it went through the back leg. He rinsed both sides and bandaged it. Geronimo had many other bite and claw marks all over his body in various degrees of severity. Ben rinsed and bandaged anything that was still bleeding. G-dog blacked out on the back seat.

"Seem like a lot of work," his driver said when he was finished.

"My only friend."

"Just so."

Ben dug into his bag and counted out her payment in €500 notes. "Is there an animal hospital in Maun?" he asked.

"Sort of. There are some people there who can help your friend."

"Good. Listen, I need some help, and I can pay. Do you know a good forger? I am in trouble, and I need some new documents to travel."

"What is in it for me? It looks like your trouble becomes my trouble if I help you anymore."

"Another five K if you get me to a professional-grade forger."

"OK, I maybe know someone. Uluthando maybe help you. Get in your car, and follow me. We drop your friend in Maun, and we leave from there."

They shook on it, with Ben still having a hard time not looking at her, despite everything. She exuded a combination of strength and femininity that was intimidating and irresistible at the same time. He wanted her protection.

"Follow me."

They both took off northwest toward the frontier town of Maun.

56

They drove on for a few hours through the African outback, Ben still periodically laying on his horn to dissuade the legions of warthogs that leaped out from the shoulder at all angles. He was getting pretty good at it. One blast of the horn and a jerk of the wheel were all it took to keep the porcine population of Botswana intact. Geronimo wasn't moving much, but he was still breathing. Ben couldn't be sure, but he thought he would make it if he could get some medical attention. *Where is Bob the vet when you need him?*

The two-lane highway finally took them to Maun. Ben's first impression was that it was similar to frontier towns everywhere: Manaus, Kathmandu, Nogales, Mos Eisley. It had that strange combination of calm and frenetic business endemic to the type of place that is both a launching point to the hinterlands and a dead end for the detritus of the worldwide adventure community—pilots, mercs, mountaineers, and so on. On the outskirts of town, Ben turned off the road, following Zak in her Mercedes, where she parked in front of a two-story Victorian building with an upper balcony that looked like it could be at home in Colorado, the Australian outback, or apparently Botswana. The ghost of empire. It looked to be some kind of saloon. She got out of her car and motioned for Ben to wait. A few minutes later, she came out with a grizzled old Afrikaner drinking a Tusker. Ben rolled down his window as they approached.

"This man is an animal doctor. He normally works on sheep, but he has agreed to help out your friend while you go meet Uluthando."

"Let's have a look at your boy, eh?" he said, walking around to the back seat. He peeled back the blanket and whistled. "How did this happen, bru?"

"Gunshot, hyena," Ben deadpanned.

"Anything else?"

"Unknown. Can you help him?"

"I reckon so. Will take a couple of days. Have him out at my farm; you can pick him up after you conclude your business with this young woman here," he said, finishing his beer, reaching in and cradling Geronimo in the blanket, and putting him in the front seat of his own beat-to-hell Land Rover pickup.

"Let's go. You drive," she said, climbing gracefully into Ben's Landy.

"OK, where are we going?" he replied, squinting as his only friend on the planet drove away with some strange rancher in a vehicle that looked like it had been scavenged for parts.

"Toward the airport. We need to meet a pilot there. He will fly us to Uluthando."

"Fly us? I didn't agree to that. Fly us where?"

"What it matter to you? You get what you want, I get paid, everybody happy. Right?"

"Right," Ben said, putting the rig in reverse and pulling backward.

They drove around for a few minutes until they found the airfield. Across the street was a rather silly-looking aviation-themed restaurant where they pulled up front and parked.

"Inside is our pilot," she said, getting out.

Ben followed her into the place, involuntarily checking out her legs in the process. She led him to a table in the back where a white man in a leather jacket stood up and hugged her. He was looking every bit the bush pilot, matching the aviation kitsch of the restaurant perfectly.

"Is this the guy?" he asked, clearly English.

"Yeah, are you willing to take him?"

"Maybe. Do you trust him?"

"I don't even know him."

"Who is after you, mate?" he asked Ben.

"Everybody. What about you?"

"After all these years, brother, hopefully nobody. OK, tell me this: How much shit am I in by helping you?"

Ben exhaled heavily.

"At this point, dude, I think I am in the clear for the moment, but no guarantees. I am not sure who all the players are, and they shot my dog."

"Fecking heathens," he muttered.

"Fair enough. I'll take you to Uluthando, but it is two thousand euros round trip, paid up front. Would be more, but I am headed that way with your friend here, so you are getting the discount rate. My name is Craig, by the way."

"Ben Adams. Where are we going?"

"We are going into the delta, mate, deep. You want a lift or not?"

"Yes, I do."

"All right, grab your kit, and let's go. Plane is out this way."

Ben grabbed his stuff from the truck, and they all walked out to the flight line where an old de Havilland Beaver on floats sat. At the flight line, Ben moved his eyes to more important things, namely the plane that was ferrying them to wherever it was they were going. Ben didn't know that much about planes, but he understood mechanical things and was perfectly fastidious about maintaining them. One glance at the plane and he could tell it was old, possibly very old, and definitely not maintained to his standard. It appeared robustly built with what Ben assumed were 1940s technology and craftsmanship. However, it had clearly had a hard life. There was no shortage of dents, stains, and other damage all over the body of the thing. Each of the floats was a different color, and neither matched the plane. Ben started to wonder how a float plane was going to take off on a runway in the desert when he noticed the little wheels under the floats. His next thought was that wherever they were headed, it was probably wet. With a vague idea that he was nowhere near the ocean, Ben had very little to work with. Craig did a quick walk-around of the plane, presumably to look for new damage.

"All right, then, everyone aboard," Craig said, peeling open the door on the side of the aircraft.

They all piled in. Ben had a small bag from his Land Rover with all his IDs, his pistol, and his cash and currency. They were not leaving his possession again if he could help it.

The old engine coughed to life with a cloud of black smoke. The pilot didn't seem bothered by it, which meant this must have been how it operated normally. He spoke rapidly into the microphone then, presumably having received clearance, throttled up and wheeled the plane out onto the runway. Brakes on, he pushed the throttle full forward, and the plane seemed to want to shake itself apart. He slipped the brakes, and the old craft rolled forward, picking up speed. At a point that Ben thought was suspiciously close to the end of the runway, the plane clumsily gained flight. Once airborne, they turned north. By this time Ben had a really good concept of the north-south thing due to his bush walk, and he wasn't going to forget it. It wasn't long before the floats on the plane started to make sense. The Kalahari quickly gave way to the Okavango Delta, and sand turned to water. Parched grassland became entirely inland sea. There were occasional islands, but the farther they went, the less obvious they were. The Okavango Delta is the terminus of the Okavango River, which starts in Angola. Every year, heavy rains in Angola flood the desert in Botswana, creating thousands of square miles where water rules for the season. As they flew, Ben asked his pilot about himself in an effort to stop thinking about his own screwed-up situation.

"Your accent sounds English. How did you end up here?"

"Yeah, well, Welsh, actually. Learned to fly Harriers in the Royal Navy so I could get out of Wales. Pretty good times, but I got sick of the so-called special relationship and their endless wars. Gave up on the whole thing, thought I would come down here, become a bush pilot for some peace and quiet. It turns out that Africa has its own endless wars."

"Really? Botswana seems pretty mellow. If it had a coastline and some surfable waves, I don't think I would ever leave," Ben said, putting into words what had been bouncing around his brain inchoate up until now.

"You're right, mate. Botswana is still neutral territory for now. Look," Craig said, pointing out of the windshield. "That is where we are headed," he finished deftly, ending the conversation as he banked the old bush plane.

It looked just like the rest of the delta except that there was a large rectangular hut on stilts standing out of the water like the giraffes they had been flying over for the last hour. It had the look and feel of a Viking longhouse, but over water and on stilts. Tied up to the hut were several fan boats and canoes like something straight out of the American South. There were way too many trees and plants poking out of the water for them to land there, so they banked away and aimed for a large empty stretch of water a few miles away. Craig buzzed the area once to scatter a couple of Cape buffalo, then turned around for his final approach. They touched down without incident and motored over to a copse of trees and bushes whose roots created a small island. Craig had Ben jump out and tie the float to the roots, then throw an anchor out of the other side, securing the plane in place. Just about the time when Ben was trying to figure out why the nameless, beautiful woman who had given him a ride had come along, several natives in *mokoro* canoes emerged from the reeds, approaching the plane. It became clear pretty quickly that they weren't there for him. The men paddling the mokoros paddled right up to the float, grinning yet deferential to the lithe woman climbing down from the plane. They were all rapidly speaking in Zulu in a manner that seemed to Ben to be about something very important. Craig the pilot unloaded her gear and Ben's into one of the canoes and then got in himself and grabbed a paddle.

"Are you comin', or you want to spend another night wit the animals?" she asked Ben, somewhat miffed that she had to interrupt her conversation to talk to this fool.

Ben jumped into the canoe behind Craig as its former operator jumped in with the rest of the natives and Ben's mysterious savior. Ben and Craig started the several-mile paddle to the longhouse. Up to this point, Ben had been so preoccupied with his own issues—dying of thirst, multiple attempts on his life, vengeance for his dog, and so on—that he had not put any of his considerable brainpower into figuring out who his host was and what exactly was going on here. Surfers sometimes have a reputation for appearing a little spacey, but that is often the result of a lifetime of disappointment in searching for good waves, the riding of which is ultimately useless and extremely fleeting. The upside is that anybody who has surfed for any length of time has had a crash course in Zen and the realization that rarely does the world give you what you want; most of the time, you just kind of have to go with it. This was where Ben was at the moment. He was paddling a canoe, in Africa, with a shell-shocked British pilot and a group of natives with a random stunning woman who appeared to be in some sort of leadership role for a group of possible African Vikings on the Okavango Delta. For Ben, very often reality didn't stand up to any form of hard scrutiny and thus had to be ignored as much as possible. Now was such a time, so Ben decided to focus on making very good and efficient paddle strokes while not thinking about the giant boa constrictor he had just seen swimming under his boat.

57

ohammed knew he was being followed. It was most likely the sniper, trying to get the nuclear triggers for himself. He would have gone where they went. Mohammed may have been old, but a one-on-one situation in the wilderness, rifle or not, he wasn't worried. He owned this situation. He just moved from cover to cover, headed north. He could find water; he could survive. Sooner or later, the wily old warrior would make it to the caliphate with his cargo, on foot if necessary.

58

en got lost in his paddle strokes. They were perfect, no wasted motion at all. The canoe was gliding silently. Occasionally Craig would look back from the front, which Ben took as affirmation that they were cruising along nicely but in reality was probably totally unrelated. The focus on the perfection of the stroke worked exactly to jar loose his thoughts and plan of action. He was way past pondering any morality of his life and his actions. Wolf Larsen was right: the world is a bad place full of killers, and you are either killer or killee, and Ben preferred being alive most of the time. His plan was to get his full set of documents with a new identity, get his dog, make his way to Cape Town, catch a boat to New Zealand to RV with Jessica and her beach batch, and live happily ever after. Fade out. Roll credits. The end. He vowed to manage his demons more effectively and do whatever it took to appreciate that scenario. It was elegant in its design. Its execution might be another story.

After about forty minutes of paddling, they pushed through the reeds, and the longhouse came into view. From the water level, it looked like some sort of Louisiana bayou shack on steroids. Same swampy wooden house on stilts, but giant, with solar cells and multiple radio and satellite antennae on the roof.

"Dude, what is this place?" Ben called forward to the pilot.

"All will be revealed, my son. Just wait and make sure that they let us in."

"*Pfffff.*"

Zak got the same reception at the longhouse as she had got at the plane: loads of deference and admiration. Ben really had no frame of reference for this but, true to form, was going with it. She spoke rapidly in Zulu and gestured to the two white men in the canoe. Ben scanned the building, keeping his antennae up for whatever terrible thing was about to befall him. Standing on the patio at the other end of the building were five hard-looking white guys in full tactical gear, with assault rifles and pistols to match. Ben had seen enough of these guys to know that he sincerely hoped they were on his side, at least for today. The Zulus at the house motioned for Ben and Craig to tie up the boat and climb up the ladder into the building. This was it. Whatever it was going to be, Ben would find out now. Ben made sure his pistol was accessible in his waistband and climbed up. Hitting the wraparound deck, Ben readied himself. Nothing happened. They motioned him inside. Once in the door, he braced for action again. Again, nothing. The room they entered had the look and feel of the lobby of a medium-size business. There were desks, chairs, coffee makers, and some sort of lounge in the corner. They even had a large flat-screen television tuned to CNN in the corner by the couches. Ben's thoughts went no further than to be grateful that he hadn't been ambushed.

"Have a seat. There is a laptop over by the television that you can use. All of our IP addresses are masked here with Tor, so even if the CIA is after you, you should be safe to check whatever you need to," Zak said, exiting the room to attend to whatever it was she did here. Craig went to the refrigerator and took out a glass bottle of Coca-Cola and held it up toward Ben. Ben nodded, and Craig grabbed a second bottle and popped the caps with an opener screwed to the wall. He walked over, handed one bottle to Ben, and then flopped down on the couch.

"Now what?" Ben asked.

"Now I am just waiting on you to finish your business here so I can take you back to Maun. I am glad I brought my book," he said, visibly relaxing and flipping open a copy of *Desert Solitaire*. Ben looked at the laptop on the coffee table and stared at it for a while. He had no idea what Tor was, but it sounded legit. He would e-mail Jessica and let her know he was coming home. Hard-looking mercs from outside kept coming and going from the building, keeping a wary eye on Ben every time they moved through the room. He glanced up at the television. Nothing showed on the news about the bloodbath at the racetrack.

59

Ben sat in the "lounge" of wherever he was and watched the news on mute. Nothing good was happening. *Is there ever?* Air Supply's greatest hits filled the background. He had fired off his e-mail to Jessica and was feeling pretty good about his plan. Another merc walked through the room looking sideways at Ben; they didn't even appear human, just machines of death. Simple killers handy with weapons and with a large tolerance for discomfort. He knew these guys. It occurred to Ben that the look he was receiving from them was possibly one of recognition of one of the same species. Ben shuddered at that and went back to fantasizing about his plan to end up back at the beach in New Zealand. This made him feel better. After about two hours, one of the armed death machines came out of a back office and, with a thick Afrikaner accent, said,

"Uluthando is ready for you. End of the hall," and walked out of the building.

Ben looked to Craig, who was thumbing through a magazine on another couch, for some sort of reaction. There was none. Ben grabbed all his stuff and headed back. He walked down a hallway, which bisected the building to the end, and walked into a partially open door. He pushed it open and walked in. At a large executive-style desk sat Zak, looking as great as ever.

"You? Zak? Uluthando?"

"Uluthando means 'She is love.' It is more of a title or nom de guerre. I need anonymity. There are a great many people who would wish my death. I am sure that you can relate," she replied.

"OK, but who is Zak?"

"Nobody, just another made-up name."

Ben ran his hands through his hair. "OK, can you help me?"

"Yes, I can. Show me what you have, Mr. Adams," she said with a formality and elocution that Ben found even more confusing.

Ben fished out his current passport and his old diplomatic passport. "If you can use these, great. Otherwise, I am happy to start from scratch."

"I have people who can create new passports, but they are expensive and take a few weeks. Based on what I have seen, I am guessing that you don't have a few weeks."

"Good guess."

"I think that my people can modify what you have in a way that will be good for any land border in Africa. We won't be able to alter the RFID chip here. If you go to an airport in Europe or the United States, it will scan your true identity, so if you need this quickly, that is all that I can do." She sat back.

"That will have to do. How much?"

"Two thousand euros, and we will have it for you tomorrow. You can sleep on the couch, and our pilot will take you back to Maun tomorrow after it is complete."

Ben counted out €2,000 and placed them on the table. Uluthando took the money and the passports and walked out of the door. She returned a moment later and said, "We will have to destroy one of the passports to use the materials, so you will end up with just one, but it will be with your picture, new name and date of birth, and fabricated passport number. It will be a very good forgery, but not perfect. Be careful, and remember, you don't know me, and we never met."

She stuck her hand out, and Ben took it. "Wait," he said. "What do you do here? What is this all about?"

"Sorry, my friend. You don't know me. I hope that your dog gets better. Now, I have much business to attend to."

She ushered him out of the door. Ben paused for a moment in the hallway, his curiosity about the nature of Uluthando and this place picking at his soul. He let it go as not germane to his current purpose of staying alive and staying out of jail and ambled back to the lobby/lounge. He grabbed another Coke and waited. He had nothing to read and nothing to do, so he just waited.

Ben hadn't realized he had nodded off. He figured the adrenaline must have worn off, and the horrors of the last few days must have caught up with him. Despite the soreness and the pain, the sleep had felt good. He looked around the room. He licked his lips and realized that he would kill for a toothbrush. Craig was sawing logs on the other couch, and no one else was around. Craig struck Ben as the kind of guy who, having spent much time in the military, was accustomed to the concept of "hurry up and wait" and thus had no problem taking advantage of food and sleep whenever the opportunity presented itself. Ben got up and found a dingy bathroom and splashed some water on his face. He looked in the mirror for the first time in a while. Not good. Right eye still half-closed and black and blue. He remembered his e-mail to Jessica and thought to check again to see if she had got back to him. It didn't really matter; he was going with his plan no matter what at this point. If she rejected him once he landed in New Zealand, he would respect that. At least he would be safely hidden on the other side of the world and could hide there forever, alone if it came down to it. He walked back to the lounge and cracked open the laptop. He logged in and saw two messages. The first was from his vet, Bob, and it was dated two days ago. He ignored it and opened the one from Jessica. It didn't have her usual teasing tone and cursing. It was direct and disturbing.

> **I heard that you are in trouble. Meet me in Cape Town in three days. Location to follow.**
>
> **—Jess**

Ben sat back, confused. *Cape Town? She was never super flowery in her language, but this is especially curt. Has Homeland Security gotten to her? Is it a trap?*

Didn't matter. He was headed to Cape Town, anyway, for his launch to New Zealand. If she was there, so much the better. They could go together; it would be an adventure, just like when they met! Ben knew that rationale was pretty thin, but it was all he had. He went back to the first e-mail message from Bob.

> **Hey bud, surf has been flat here, hope South Africa has been treating you well. Remember to reach out if you need anything.**
>
> **—Bob**

Another strange e-mail. Bob wasn't exactly the type to send a superficial communication; it was one of

the things Ben liked about him. Maybe he was looking for enemies where there weren't any, chasing
ghosts. He might be just way too wired after all the
shit that had happened. Fatigued with no easy answers, he lay back on the couch and fell back into a
deep sleep.

Ben awoke in what he presumed was the morning.
There was sunlight streaming in through the windows,
and there were people busily attending to whatever it
was, in fact, that went on here. He rubbed his face as
the world came into focus. Air Supply was still rocking
in the background. Craig rolled in from somewhere
else with two cups of coffee.

"Welcome back, mate," he said, holding out a cup.

Ben had never been so thankful for anything in all
his life. On top of the physical assaults and the nearly
dying in the wilderness, Ben had been without coffee
for several days, and his addiction had been making
itself known with ferocious intensity.

"Looks like your docs ought to be ready in about
thirty minutes. You ready to go after that?"

Ben stared into his cup. "Absolutely. Let's go."

He mentally prepared for the next leg. Canoe to
plane. Plane to Maun. Get G-dog. Cape Town. Jessica?
Boat. New Zealand. Happily ever after. Easy.

Admittedly, the later parts of the plan were a little
hazy, but he would tighten up those details as he approached them. He opened the laptop and logged into
his e-mail again. Something from Jessica.

Meet me at the Umoya Lodge in Capetown on Thursday at noon. See ya there!

—Jess.

Ben looked it up online. Seemed like some sort of surf hostel. This lent credence to the e-mail, but it definitely still didn't seem quite right. It was her e-mail address, but it could have been hacked.

Maybe she didn't notice? She is in academia. She checks it all the time. She would probably notice.

Ben didn't have any good answers, just more questions. He put a mental pin in the location and time of the meet and would reevaluate when he got there. Maybe get a room a day early and scope out the situation in advance.

That's it.

He did a quick search looking for news about the track murders. Nothing. Somebody cleaned it up. That put a small glimmer of hope in Ben's mind that if he just disappeared, nobody would come looking. It was admittedly pretty thin, but it was something. He finished his coffee and waited. It wasn't long before Craig came out of a doorway with an envelope in his hands. He tossed it onto Ben's lap. Ben opened it up and found a lovely blue US passport and the shredded remains of his old diplomatic passport. He opened it up and saw his familiar mug in what appeared at first glance to be his original passport. Upon closer inspection, he noticed that the number was different, and his name was no longer Ben Adams but now Ren Adamson, with a DOB three years and three months younger than his original. Ben had never worked for the State Department, but it seemed like a class-A passport forgery, and he was glad to get it. Also included were handwritten driving directions to the farm where Geronimo had been taken for treatment. He grabbed the rest of his stuff, looked up at Craig, and said, "I'm ready."

"Right. I'll get one of the guys to take us back to the plane. Meet you outside at the launch."

Ben nodded assent and got up and walked out of the front door. Outside on the balcony, he squinted into the light. He was near the ladder that led down to the boat launch, so he just leaned on the railing and took in the wonder that is the Okavango Delta. In the distance he could see some elephants walking knee-deep in the water, eating as they went. A colorful bee-eater zoomed around. In the right context, this was another paradise. But just like in all the other ones, Ben was feeling imprisoned. He tried to weigh how much of that was the actual circumstances and how much was his own mental baggage. The smell of cigarette smoke broke his train of thought. He looked down the railing to the other end of the building. The mercenaries from yesterday were all milling around. They were still in full tactical gear and fully armed.

They looked like a bunch of hammers looking for a nail. Ben turned away and refocused on the nonhuman wildlife. Craig came up from behind and slapped him on the back.

"This is Kagiso. He will be taking us back in his Makoro," he said, indicating one of the boatmen from yesterday.

Kagiso slowly waved as he climbed down the ladder to the waiting canoe. Ben followed with Craig right behind. They wobbled into the canoe and set off. The mercs watched them leave with feigned disinterest. It was clearly not a free ride as there were three paddles in the canoe, so Ben and Craig picked up two and started pulling their weight.

"OK, dude, what the fuck is going on there? What is that place, and who is Uluthando?" Ben asked as soon as they were out of earshot of the stilted building.

"It's a lot to unpack, Ben. Not sure where to start," Craig said from the back of the canoe.

"Just give me the highlights. I am a quick study."

"OK, Angola isn't exactly what you would call stable, right?" He continued without waiting for an answer. "There is a simmering civil war up there, mate, and there are three main factions at this point. There are actually hundreds of factions that shift on a daily basis; it is a total fucking disaster. The oil interests and the diamond cartel have the government in their pockets and are trying to open up as much territory as they can for their operations. This puts them at serious odds with the people who actually live there and the people trying to conserve what is left of the wildlife and wilderness. Certain factions in the army are actually in open war against the civil government in an effort to bring back the wildlife and turn Angola's economy into a tourist-based one as opposed to an extractive one, which the government wants. The natives are just trying to get through the day. They have the bulldozers of the miners and oil guys on one hand trying to blade their homes and the conservationists on the other hand trying to kick them out of the jungle. Bushmeat and poaching for the Chinese medicine market are usually the only way they can survive."

"OK, so that makes the place we left some sort of revolutionary base? For what?"

"Uluthando is on the conservation side. She is using diamonds brought by her contacts all over Africa to finance the conservation of as much of the wilderness in Angola as she can. She hires the natives to protect the land that they are already on, thereby turning enemies into assets, swords into ploughshares, or bushmeat into chicken coops, as it were. The Angolan government has a one-million-US-dollar bounty on her head."

"What about the guys on the deck outside the building?"

"Mercenaries from an outfit from the States called Bear Claw Global Logistics or some shite like that. Total arseholes, if you ask me, but I guess they are our arseholes. They train the guys we hire, kill the poachers if necessary, and sabotage the mining and oil guys' operations, something like your Monkey Wrench Gang in the United States. They are mostly burned-out Iraq and Afghanistan vets."

Ben's blood ran cold at the mention of Bear Claw. He wondered if he would ever get clear of this fucking company.

"Our assholes? Are you in on this?"

"I am bought and paid for just like the mercs. I believe in the struggle, mate. I really do, but I guess it just seems hopeless to me. No winning it down here, you know? Still, as long as I can keep food on the table and don't get a better offer, I am going to stay with her."

"You are a true romantic, bro."

"Go to hell, mate. Spend more than three minutes in Africa, and then you can lecture me."

"Fair enough," Ben said as they kept rowing.

As he rowed, his turned his thoughts to the Bear Claw guys. Surely it was a coincidence; those death merchants had to be everywhere around the globe. Ben was not a huge fan of coincidences. The question was, did they know who he was? And if so, would they care? It was a huge company with guys deployed around the world; the odds that those guys would have known that Ben Adams had killed some of their guys two years ago and then linked it up with the Ben Adams who just rowed away from their redoubt in the Okavango Delta were pretty low, right?

Ben put it at 25 percent, maybe 35 given the streak he was on. Low enough not to affect his decision-making at this point.

They got back to the sad-looking de Havilland and sent the boatman on his way with a wave. As the pilot looked around the plane, Ben slipped special agent Goodman's credentials into the water, the badge reflecting sunlight as it sank. With his new identity, it was the last physical piece of evidence connecting him to the dead man and the botched operation. Both of the white guys climbed aboard and settled into the seats as Craig went through his preflight routine. He worked very professionally and methodically, which made Ben feel a bit better about the plane. Perhaps it was like his old jeep? Neglected on the outside but shining like a gem underneath. Ben decided believing that was the case was his most prudent course of action as they were going to be airborne in a moment, and all the worrying in the world wasn't going to add any lift to those wings. Craig motored it out onto open water and into the breeze. He throttled up, and they raced forward through the shallow delta, scattering birds as they went. Mercifully, they all flew out of the way, and quickly the plane was airborne. As they rapidly gained altitude, Ben looked at the beauty and remoteness of the delta. Besides Uluthando's HQ, there didn't seem to be any human intrusion. He liked that.

They made it back to Maun and landed. Craig taxied them over to a hangar and killed the engine.

"You want to get a beer, mate?" Craig asked as they got out of the plane.

"Gotta get my dog,"

"Understood. Take care, and good luck," Craig said, extending his hand.

Ben shook it with genuine pleasure. He had been so consumed by fear and hate lately that he hadn't paid much attention to the people who had helped keep him alive for the past few days. He recognized it now as he looked at the war-weary pilot and wished he could get that beer with him just then, but he had to go. He had a plan. Ben took his new passport and his cash and went back to his Land Rover. He approached slowly and at an oblique angle. He was back in the real world that was currently trying to kill him, and he needed to bring his tactics back up. Nothing seemed amiss. The Rover was just a bit dustier. A quick scan revealed no overt surveillance. Ben got in and started it up. All systems working. He unfolded the map to the ranch and started backing out of the parking space. An old Peugeot raced in behind him and stopped suddenly, blocking him in. Ben went for his gun, reached around, and started to raise it as the driver of the Peugeot waved an apology, put down her phone, and reversed into another space, clearly just not paying attention. Ben exhaled, put down the gun, and got out of the parking lot and onto the main road. He linked up with the highway and drove 2.2 kilometers and turned right into the bush as the map indicated. Another 30 kilometers down the road and he found the farm. It looked to Ben like a sheep ranch, and so it was. He let himself in the main gate and drove up to the house. A gang of dogs came out to greet him, including one limping, shaved, bandaged, but remarkably healthy-looking Geronimo. Ben got out of the car and gave his dog a huge embrace. He was simultaneously dogpiled by the rest of the gang, and he rolled backward into the dirt. He didn't care; he was enjoying this moment and was definitely preferring canine company to that of humans, so he just lay back and took the snouts, licks, claws, and bites.

"Whoooo, your old boy came back nicely, eh?" the old farmer said, coming out of the house.

Ben extricated himself from the pile, grinning, and said, "He sure did. I owe you many thanks."

"'Twas easy. Your boy did the hard work. Biltong? Beer?"

"Yes. Yes."

Ben followed as the man hoisted himself up the steps of the ranch house and inside. The place had to be at least a hundred years old but appeared to be kept in perfect condition. Ben wanted to ask about the place but, knowing enough about southern Africa's history, chose not to. Craig was right: he was swimming in waters he did not truly understand. *Stay focused.* Ben followed the sheep man into the kitchen, where he sat on a stool at the counter. The man brought out some very good beef jerky and produced a Tusker in a bottle as well. Ben agreed to the biltong because it came with beer. He hadn't known what he agreed to eat. He learned only then that biltong was the South African version of jerky and that it was terrific, more so with beer. Geronimo had come inside and sat next to Ben. He gave his grateful dog some of the biltong, and for that moment, all was right in the world. He drained his beer quickly. He wanted to linger, but the plan was still in place. No sense in wasting time.

Ben started to get up from the stool.

"You and your boy want to stay the night? It will be dark soon, and lots of animals on the road at this hour."

"Thanks, man, but we have to get going south. Have a boat to catch."

Ben reached into his pocket and put a wad of South African rand on the counter.

"That is not necessary, Ben, truly."

"It absolutely is," Ben said with a look that didn't allow for any negotiation. "Thanks again," he said as he and Geronimo walked outside and toward the Rover. Geronimo wasn't quite up to jumping in the front seat just yet, so Ben helped him up. Ben got in himself, and they drove off. Ben smiled for the first time in a long time. Gaining the highway, they drove west, looking to hook up with the highway heading south back into South Africa and toward Cape Town.

60

en was feeling pretty confident as they drove on. The sun was getting low, and he started to think about where they would sleep that night. He still had plenty of food in the rig, and with the rooftop tent, they could post up anywhere they liked. Ben liked to make camp before dark as it was easier to set up, so he started halfway looking for presentable spots. Squinting into the sun, Ben saw what appeared to be some traffic ahead. His brain quickly realized as he approached that it was a roadblock made by three Land Rovers very similar to what he was driving, and on the other side of the trucks, he could see the faces of the Bear Claw guys from the delta peering over their M4s at him.

I guess that answers that, he thought as he slammed on the brakes, pulled his pistol, shifted into reverse, and then started firing out of the right-hand window and blasting backward at full speed.

Being right-handed, Ben finally found the one advantage to having the steering wheel on the wrong side of the car. He emptied his magazine out of the window and saw at least three of his rounds connect with their targets as his windshield exploded in cracks. He couldn't be sure about the other shots. He threw the empty pistol in his lap as he gripped the wheel with both hands and whipped it right. It spun the car backward into the bush, and he reversed into the Kalahari at max speed. He was making lots of dust, which would make him easy to follow but hard to shoot. Ben had no idea how close they were, but he couldn't see them, so he took a chance. He flung the wheel again and, executing a perfect J-turn, got the Land Rover turned and pointed forward. They bounded through the desert, weaving between the acacias, looking for something approximating a trail. With the dust he couldn't see them, but he could hear the occasional crack of a rifle, so he knew they were back there. The four-cylinder diesel of the Land Rover wasn't exactly built for speed, and it seemed as if at least one of his tires was losing air. This chase was going to come to a conclusion one way or another rather quickly.

Ben kept the hammer down, weaving between the trees and scaring the wildlife when all of a sudden the trail cleared and went as smooth as freshly laid concrete. For about four airborne seconds. They landed hard in the dry riverbed, having launched from the bank and fallen about fifteen feet. Geronimo seemed OK in the passenger footwell, although Ben thought he saw an accusatory glance thrown in his direction. Ben looked out of the window and saw his pursuers skid to a stop at the cliff's edge. Perhaps vengeance and robbery weren't motivation enough to fly off the cliff with him. But they were apparently still worth shooting for. The doors flew open, and the entire Bear Claw gang started firing wildly before their boots even hit the ground. Not waiting for their aim to improve, Ben put his foot down again, hoping for a response. Somehow the Land Rover reacted and lurched forward down the riverbed.

Maybe the British army was on to something with these things.

The front end was getting sloppy, either from a flat tire or possibly something worse, and steam started to come out from under the hood, but Ben kept it floored until he was sure they were out of the kill zone. After about a mile down the riverbed, Ben pulled up against the canyon wall and turned off the truck. He hoped he hadn't fried the engine; he wasn't really up for another death march through the Kalahari. The vegetation approaching the banks of the riverbed looked too dense to drive a vehicle through, so Ben thought he had a 75 percent chance that he was out of the woods for the moment. Those assholes hopefully weren't motivated enough to ditch their rigs and follow him on foot. He got out and listened. No motor sounds. He checked on Geronimo. Pretty good shape considering. He let the dog out of the car, and despite his limp, G-dog seemed happy to walk around a bit and smell some stuff. Ben set a bowl of water out for him and surveyed his vehicle. The results were encouraging. All glass shot to hell, two flat tires, and two small .223-size holes in his radiator, as well as many same-size holes in the body. Ben could work with this. He quickly replaced both tires. Two spares was SOP for the African bush, and luckily, both of Ben's were still intact. Ben knocked out the most egregiously shattered windows. All that was left was the radiator. Ben had spent enough time cruising Baja California in an old jeep to know that a radiator problem in the desert often meant life or death. He had heard but never confirmed that coffee grounds poured into a radiator would swim around and fill up the holes. Some dude in Pacific Beach had told Ben that he fixed his radiator this way on an old scout in Mainland Mex, and the repair lasted five years.

Not wanting to reveal his position in case the Bear Claw guys were on foot and listening, Ben found some brush, cut it down, and did a mediocre job of camouflaging the Land Rover until dark, when he would work on the radiator. He looked at his surfboard on the roof; it had also sustained some damage. He took it down, and for no other reason than to satisfy his OCD personality, he duct-taped the bullet holes. The fact that he was hundreds of miles away from the ocean and fleeing for his life from any number of government assassins and mercenaries didn't matter. He just couldn't leave the surfboard alone. It had to be tended to. He re-racked the board after he finished; took one last look around; and satisfied that he was apparently alone, got in the car, reloaded his pistol, cranked the seat back, and went to sleep, his body collapsing after the latest crest of adrenaline.

Several hours later, Ben wiggled awake. It was well past sundown. Had he heard something? Probably not. Geronimo would have said. He slowly opened the door and quietly rolled out of the passenger seat and winced in pain as his feet hit the ground. G-dog came up to him wagging, having just returned from some sort of adventure. Apparently, the bullet wound and near killing by the hyenas had done little to dampen his spirit. Dogs were good that way. Ben walked around, stopping every few steps to listen. Reasonably satisfied again, Ben fired up the Rover. He let it warm up for a second, watching the water spill out of the bullet holes in his radiator. He felt like once he started making noise, the clock was ticking. Once sufficiently warm, he started dumping the last of his coffee into the radiator, then filled the rest with water from his cooler and watched as the volume of water hitting the sand got smaller and smaller until it stopped completely. He considered putting a cup underneath for some outback safari brew but thought better of it. Ben topped off with water, and he was ready to go.

Ben dug around in his gear for the handheld GPS unit he had bought during his buying spree in Johannesburg. He found it and held it up. It had suffered a fatal gunshot wound with clear entry and exit. He dug around some more until he found a paper map of Botswana. He had only the vaguest notion of where he was. By process of elimination, he figured he was hemmed in by the Okavango to the north and the east. To the south by Highway A3, which he was on when he had been ambushed, and to the west by Highway A35. The dry riverbed he was in was pointed west-ish, so if he stayed in the river, quite possibly sooner or later he would hit one of those roads.

His dashboard compass was still functioning, so he would know which way to turn. Not wanting to run with his lights on (the ones that still worked, anyway), Ben dug out the night-vision goggles that were bought on a lark but that were suddenly very important. Mercifully, they had escaped gunfire, and Ben's world turned green as he put them on and fired them up. Geronimo, enjoying the new windshield-less Land Rover, put his paws on the dash and stuck his head through the now empty space, sticking his nose straight into the breeze so as not to miss any new scents. Ben put the rig in gear and set out, slowly. He wasn't sure what other mechanical systems were just barely hanging on at this point. They crept down the river at around five miles an hour. Ben wasn't used to NVGs, and the lack of depth perception was messing with him. Five miles an hour was all he could manage, no matter what shape the car was in. G-dog, however, was in his element. Ben could see the starlight reflect sharply off the dog's eyes in what must have been a very useful adaptation for his previous life as a street dog in La Paz.

Onward they crawled through the night. Periodically, Ben would spot pairs of glowing eyes looking down on them from atop the high banks of the riverbed. Ben was unconcerned with the nocturnal predators of the Kalahari; he had been the subject of so many murder attempts at this point that the thought of ending up as animal poop seemed downright pleasant by comparison. The Rover had no trouble with the sand, and they encountered no major obstacles. They once had to winch a fallen tree out of the way, but that was accomplished without incident. They kept on until dawn when they came to a road crossing the river. Botswana infrastructure being what it is, there was no bridge, and the pavement went straight across the river with a series of small pipes underneath to let the water go through. Luckily, the pavement was low enough that the Defender could creep right up the bank and onto the road. He was on the pavement; his plan was intact. He could still do this. He had a new intermediate goal, which was to get back to South Africa today and alive. He would worry about the rest later. He checked his compass and made a left onto what he assumed was the A35 southbound. Just a few hundred miles. He hoped his rig would make it.

61

en's Land Rover was working well enough. The radiator seemed to be holding, and the tires still held air. There was a series of new vibrations running through the rig, but considering what it had been through, that seemed fair. It also pulled sharply to the left under braking and pulled moderately to the right the rest of the time, but all things considered, it was working quite well. They trekked south toward the South African border. Ben was worried about what the border officials would think of his vehicle and whether that would invite any extra scrutiny of his passport.

They approached the border crossing near Lobatse. As soon as he saw the cement shacks and the line of trucks waiting to cross, he relaxed a little bit. Whether or not his passport made it through, his truck wasn't going to get a second glance. It wasn't even the most jacked-up vehicle there. It was like a secondhand car lot for *Mad Max* rejects. Ben parked, told Geronimo to stay, and went into the building. More bad movie scenes. An unpainted cinder-block interior with a slowly rotating ceiling fan. A hard-looking woman working the desk. Ben got in line. He was third. He used this time to watch the process and look for electronics.

Will she scan the RFID? If she does, will she notice the different name? Is Interpol all over this shit? Relax, Ben; it is going to be what it is going to be.

When his time came, he went up to the counter. It was warm, so his sweating didn't look that unusual. He put down his passport and sent it across. The woman picked it up quickly and looked for the visa stamp from his entry and noted something down on her desk. She flipped to the photo and compared it to Ben. He gave a crooked smile that was the best he could muster. She put the passport down and stamped it.

"Welcome back to South Africa, Mr. Adamson."

Ben thanked her quickly and bolted out of there. He turned the key in the Land Rover, and it groaned. He could hear the flywheel slowly turn as it eventually caught and sputtered to life, spewing white smoke out of the back. Ben eased across the border where the Customs people just waved him in. Ben continued south toward the Cape. He stopped for fuel in the diamond center of Kimberley. There weren't that many highways in this country; Bear Claw had to be right behind him. Ben got back into his demolished vehicle thinking about Cecil Rhodes and the ambition to paint Africa in British Red. It seemed like Bear Claw wanted it painted in Ben Adams Red. Ben's mood darkened even further, which he hadn't thought was possible. He kept an eye on his rearview mirror, waiting for the inevitable attack. He drove on, ready to hammer through another roadblock. He figured he had maybe one more good fight in him, physically and mentally. He was holding on to the very thin thread that was his plan. Him, Geronimo, Jessica, New Zealand. Still very far away but not impossible. The pieces were there. He would know pretty quickly how it was going to go down once he got to Cape Town.

He drove for hours, Geronimo sleeping next to him, not bothered by the lack of a windshield. Ben took the occasional bug in the face, but after his week, he didn't even notice. By the time they got to Cape Town, Ben was trashed. He needed to sleep. He would do his best to maintain situational awareness, but he was fading fast. He worked his way through town, through the shantytowns of the outskirts, asking for directions every few miles in the townships that were so riddled with poverty and crime that his stopping amounted to the riskiest thing he had done so far, but his GPS was shot, and he was running out of steam. Directed to the northwest part of town, he rolled past his hotel/ RV point. He did two laps around the block as coun- tersurveillance. It looked clean. Ben fully realized he was approaching full ineffectiveness, but he still had to try. He parked half a block away and took the most valuable things out of his windowless Rover, knowing full well that anything not nailed down in there would be gone tomorrow.

He walked into the lobby and leaned his surfboard against the wall. A long-haired German checked him in. Ben had never met this man, but he knew him. He could be found in San Diego, Taghazout, Tamarindo, any place where there were waves and weed. He didn't seem to judge Ben too harshly, but he was definitely a little older and a little harder than the usual surf-lodge customer. It was a charming hostel centered with rooms around a pool, but the German directed Ben around the corner to a small cottage where he would be staying. Ben asked about beer, and the German, sensing dire need, broke him off three Castle Lagers from his stash in the office. Ben and Geronimo dragged themselves around the corner and into the cottage. He set up a water bowl for G-dog with some food as well. He sat down in the provided chair and drained his first Castle in one go. The suds ran down his parched throat, and he felt the cold hit his stomach. He had a vague memory of a meat pie somewhere on the road but couldn't be sure when he had last eaten, and the beer hit his brain pretty fast. This was good. Beer, surf hotel—this was familiar. Ben couldn't be sure that he had ever been truly happy, but the closest he had ever got was in environments like this. He closed his eyes and smiled, taking a long pull on Castle number two.

Geronimo curled up at his feet and grunted as he went to sleep. Ben finished his next two beers and slept in his chair. In the back of his mind, he knew that it was insane, but for the moment he felt safe.

62

en woke up when a beam of sunshine snuck through the blinds and hit his face. Somehow he was in the bed; he must have migrated from the chair during the night. He felt almost refreshed and wasn't in his usual fit of fear and rage that his recent mornings had started with. Geronimo was already up and about. Ben walked over to the door and let him outside to handle his business. At this point he had very little doubt about Geronimo's survival instincts and knew he could handle the Cape Town beachfront. Ben walked over to the bathroom and brushed his teeth. When was the last time he had done that?

Gross.

He was supposed to meet Jessica in the office tomorrow, so he had some time. He wasn't sure if it was the familiar surfy vibe or maybe that he was close to the port where the boats were, but Ben was mellowing out. He dug out some board shorts, a T-shirt, and flip-flops. The uniform of the surf obsessed worldwide. He found Geronimo being loved on by some young and pretty backpacker types hanging out at the pool. He waved to them, and Geronimo let loose a short yap, which Ben took to mean that he was on his own for a while.

Good dog.

Ben found a coffee cart on the street and got the largest, most absurd coffee drink they would make him. He wasn't sure of the exact conversion rate, but it had to be ten bucks. They called it a Cape Macchiato Shark Feeder, and it made a pumpkin spice latte look like something you would feed a baby. He cruised along the waterfront and took in the scene. It was like beachfronts the world over: houses, apartment blocks, and hotels crowding the shoreline, the density falling rapidly with each block away from the water. He could see Table Mountain in the distance, the singular feature of Cape Town. Drawing in his breath, the humidity and temperature felt familiar; it was just like San Diego. No wonder there were so many South Africans there. Turning toward the ocean, Ben thought there looked to be some decent surf running. It was a beachbreak, but there were some rideable peaks with around half a dozen guys about a mile away. Ben knew Cape Town's reputation for great white sharks but figured it was worth the risk. He trotted back to the cottage and grabbed his board. He threw the old blue board in the car and drove down to where he had seen the other surfers. He heard the dreadlocked American girl working the morning shift at the front desk say the water temp was in the low sixties. Not exactly warm, but Ben was going to trunk it. He needed a cleanse. It felt very natural after all the violence, blood, and dust—just a man and his board going into the ocean.

Damn right.

He easily paddled out to the lineup and nodded to a couple of the locals. Maybe it was the large bruises on his torso starting to turn yellow, but everybody out there pretty much kept to themselves. The surf was about chest high with clean conditions, a perfect easy day. He caught some tiny barrels, made a cutback or two, and even got a cheater five on one particularly fast wave. His blue board also didn't seem to be taking on any water from the bullets, which was nice. After a few hours, he was starting to get thirsty and decided to call it a day. He caught a small one in and drove back toward the hostel. The sun was getting closer to the horizon, and the light was getting that nice orange afternoon glow. It might have been helped by the endorphins, but everything for once seemed to be humming right along. Ben picked up Geronimo at the pool and cruised back to his little cottage. Ben wiggled the key in the lock to his hut and opened the door and froze. Across the room in the darkness sat a man holding Ben's gun. Geronimo sprinted toward the figure. He landed in his lap and went to work on his face, licking like crazy. The figure put down the gun and gave him a big hug.

"How are you, boy? It is great to see you too, bud!"

"Jesus Christ, Bob. What the fuck are you doing here?" Ben said, exasperated that his post-surf buzz was definitely coming to a close.

"I am here to see you, man. We need to talk."

"I can't imagine that this is good news."

Ben deadpanned as he took off his wet shorts. "OK, what?" he said from the bathroom, digging out some dry clothes.

"OK, so Jessica isn't coming. I asked her to send that message to get you here."

Ben wasn't surprised; it had seemed too good to be true. "Yeah, OK. Lay it on me," he said, coming back into the room, just now noticing that Bob had an open twelve-pack of beer next to his chair. Ben reached in and took one as he made his way to the couch.

"This is the deal, bro: I know all about your deal with the FBI and Homeland Security, and I know all about Trentino and his deal for the triggers."

"What do you mean, man? I don't get it."

"You idiot. Trentino is our asset."

Ben gave him a blank look.

"CIA. Dude. Asset. We have been working him the whole time."

Ben reached into his duffel bag and pulled out the stained and torn business card of Bruce Brown, picked up on the megayacht in Monte Carlo Harbor.

"You are Bruce Brown? That was your business card! I remember now: you CIA idiots used those bullshit cards all the time. I couldn't figure out where I knew that shitty card from. What is with that, anyway?"

"Nothing crazy, just cheap cover. We make them in the office. No sense in printing tons of business cards if you need a new name every month."

"Makes sense, I guess," said Ben, a little disappointed after the high of figuring something out for once.

"I have been CIA since 9/11. I joined up after the towers went down. I was in my last year of veterinary school, and they thought that would be a good cover, so we went with that. I went to Afghanistan to ostensibly look after the army's bomb dogs, which I did and ran ops on the side. I was with the group that had bin Laden cornered in Tora Bora, but you know how that worked out."

"So you have been CIA the whole time that I have known you?"

"Pretty much. After Afghanistan, I just work part-time on special deals like this one."

"What about your dope dealing? Don't you supply weed to the whole west side of San Diego?"

"Dude, it is the CIA, not Sunday school. Dope is so eighties; at this point it is terrorism or nothing. In five years, they are going to be putting THC in the water."

"Fucking great, so I have been under surveillance by the CIA ever since you have known me?" shrieked Ben, fumbling for his beer, his paranoia pegging the needle.

"No, no, no. As far as I know, before this you were totally out, normal civilian, et cetera. They brought me into this operation because of you. This was someone else's deal, but once you got roped in, they put me on it to make sure things didn't get out of control," Bob reassured him.

"How did that turn out?"

Bob laughed. "Could have been worse, actually. Intelligence ops are usually total shit shows."

"What would you call this?"

"Medium grade at best. The bad guy is still in play; we still have a handle on it. You should have seen Afghanistan."

"OK, spell it out for me, please. If I am going to die for this, I'd like to hear it all."

"Sure, but FYI, you are not dead yet."

Ben looked down and waved his hand, telling him to skip to the good stuff.

"Trentino's dad worked for the Italian resistance when he was a teenager. He was actually at Monte Casino; the guy was a legend. So after the war, Italy was such a disaster, he emigrated to San Francisco and started an electronics firm. He used his old contacts from the war to start getting government contracts, and his whole business grew from there."

"What does that have to do with dead Goodman and almost-dead Adams?"

"Well, so when Mohammed Qureshi sent his RFP, Trentino reached out to one of his dad's old CIA contacts from the Wild Bill Donovan days, and we spun up the operation. The goal was to follow the triggers to the weapons lab and take out the whole thing with a Daisy Cutter or a MOAB, thereby destroying the fledgling ISIS nuclear program. We have a tracker stashed in with the nuclear triggers; we have been on it the whole time. Trentino does his public duty and gets to clean off a couple of mil in the process. Everybody wins. Sort of. Except the guys in the bunker."

"Fuck me."

"Sorry, bro."

"Why not bring in the FBI and DHS on this? We could have all worked together," he said wearily, going for another beer.

"No offense, bud, but giving this to the regular feds would be like giving a gun to a three-year-old. The proof is in the pudding: you guys have one agent dead, another on the run, and no idea where the triggers are."

"What? The CIA is perfect? I seem to remember some spectacular failures, something about an exploding cigar for Castro?"

Bob smiled wistfully. "That was a good one, but tell me what you know about our spectacular successes."

"What spectacular successes?"

"We did get Bin Laden. In fact Cairo, the malanois on that raid is one of my canine patients."

"Bin Laden was done on credit for screwing that up the first time. What else?"

"We operate in secret bro. No one will ever know the good we do. I would say that the fact that there isn't a worldwide radioactive ash cloud and that there is still a liberal Western order is evidence enough of our spectacular success. Fair?" he said, high on his soapbox, the beer working its way through him as well. "Not to mention, you clowns aren't really part of the intelligence community, so you have no idea."

Ben wasn't sure he liked being labeled as "you clowns." He was a fucking civilian now, but for some reason he took umbrage on behalf of the agencies he used to work for and was being currently blackmailed by.

"'Intelligence community.' God, I hate that fucking term. You make it sound like you are all part of the same homeowner's association, when meanwhile you are stepping on each other's toes and repeatedly fucking each other over, leaving a huge body count in your wake," he went on, unraveling a bit.

"Listen, dude, we aren't in *Pee-wee's Playhouse*; we are all playing by big-boy rules here with big-boy consequences, and before you give me your babe-in-the-woods routine, know that I have seen your file, and I have personally stitched up some of the bullet wounds in your body. Not to mention, I have heard your bullshit killing-club routine when you are trying to pick up chicks at the West End. Guess what, Chachi. You are right: there is a killing club, and you are neck-deep in it. I am in it. The Iraqi general is in it, and

Goodman was in it. In fact, the only asshole in this whole deal who isn't in it is Trentino."

Ben looked down, chastened. He took another drag on his beer and noticed a box of cigarettes on the counter. He took one out and lit it, inhaling deeply.

"So where is Trentino? Did he win the race?"

"Took third. Not too bad. We have him in a safe house in Johannesburg. After he found Goodman and the dead Korean, he totally freaked out, keeps going on and on about witness protection and changing his identity. We will post him up in an apartment in Fargo, North Dakota, for a while until he gets bored with all the secrecy, gets sick of eating Chinese takeout, and needs to get laid, and then we'll dump him back in the Bay Area."

"His deal didn't go. Won't he be bankrupt?"

"Honestly, Ben, the way things play out never ceases to amaze me. With Trentino gone on this adventure, his COO has been running things, and that guy got a call from someone at ICE. Turns out with the new administration planning to deport millions of people, they need more jets. They are going to use the existing aviation infrastructure that Trentino has running people out to Area 51 to shuttle all of the mass deportees coming down the pike. Called Janet Airways or something like that. Got a no-bid, sole source contract. Guy is going to make millions; his company is back. Unbelievable."

Ben closed his eyes and finished the cigarette in one go, the world going swimmy around him. He couldn't fucking believe one of PB Phil's fucked-up conspiracy theories was again messing with his real life.

"So you guys still have the triggers?" Ben said, eyes still closed.

"Our tracker is still transmitting, and our man is still following him."

"The sniper in the desert?"

"Yep. You are welcome, by the way. That old general was going to kill you had my guy not intervened. That was off the books. We had orders only to follow."

"You know I nearly died right after that in the desert. It would have been for nothing."

"You would have had one more day of life."

"Touché. How many other of your people have been on this? The private-jet pilots?"

"Yep."

"Stewardess?"

"She's great, isn't she?"

Ben started to see the big picture. "What about the girl who gave me the boat ride in Monte Carlo?"

"Rising star in the agency. Trentino was getting skittish in Monaco after you whacked his girlfriend, so we called her in to calm him down. She has a great future in intelligence work."

"Intelligence work? Is that what that was called in the stateroom on the boat?"

"Don't start, Ben. You know how the game is played. She did it for her country. I actually think she enjoyed that one."

"What about the guy who came into the container at the racetrack?"

"Oh yeah. He's ours. Nice kid, but just a little green, right out of the SEAL teams. He didn't trust the transmitter, wanted to get eyes on the triggers. He was under orders to hang back, but he was too jumpy. He almost caught one of your bullets for it too. Had to send him home. He is going to sit on the beach while management figures out what to do with him. Probably just a letter in the file, kid is good, just needs to mellow out."

"That's why his room at the hotel was empty."

"Yep, and by the way, nice job on the naked hallway improvisation. That was some great stuff! The story and the hotel surveillance video have already made the rounds at Langley. I don't think there is a spook in the Western Hemisphere who hasn't seen it. I thought I walked between the raindrops, but that was fucking gold. Truth be told, I wish we had met before you joined the feebs; I could have used you at the agency."

"Thanks. What about the bartender that night? She yours?"

"Nope, that was all you. Good job."

"What about the bush pilot?"

"What bush pilot?"

"Never mind. Who was the ninja who killed Goodman?"

"North Korean superspy. We have been after him for years—CIA code name, well, Ninja."

"Clever."

"Yeah, well, somehow they got onto the deal and wanted the triggers for their own program, and lucky for us, you took him out. Sorry about Goodman, by the way. He was a good agent and a good, well, you know."

"Yeah, well maybe you can give him a little star on your wall at Langley."

"He knew the risks, man."

"So where does that leave us?"

"My operation continues. We just got approval to-day for twenty-four-hour drone surveillance on the package starting tomorrow, so as long as our guy stays on the general and our tracker keeps transmitting un-til tomorrow, we are good to go."

"What about me?"

"You had better have another beer."

63

Mohammed watched the man's eyes bulge as he gasped for air that would never come.

"Memento mori," he whispered to the dying man lying on his back in the desert.

It had taken two days to get the drop on him, but sneaking up on people in the desert was right in his wheelhouse. Once he had the guy convinced that he had a routine, it was fairly easy for Mohammed to fake his bivouac and circle around behind him in the dark. It had taken more than the usual force to break his neck; he had had to throw his entire body weight behind the project. He was getting old for this kind of work, and this guy was a killer. He rightly guessed CIA. At this point he was immune to the pleasures or the guilt that came with killing, but it felt good to take a CIA piece off the board permanently. He had to hand it to him: he was on foot, just like Mohammed. No vehicle, no obvious air support, he had been matching him footstep for footstep across the plains, like so many wildebeest heading north. He was, however, better supplied. Qureshi took his food, water, firearms, cash, radio, and hat. Once he had known that he was being followed, he figured there had to be a tracker somewhere in the duffel bag with the krytrons, but he didn't want to tip his hand until his follower was dispatched. It took him only a few minutes to find the combination GPS and burst transmitter. He plucked it out and stuck it in the dead man's mouth as a little insult to whoever would eventually come. He double-checked both bags for a redundant transmitter, then checked everything he had taken from the commando. He was going to be hiking pretty heavy, but with the resources at his hand, he figured he would be back in ISIS territory within thirty days. Even if he had to walk the entire way, he would get there within a few months. He then realized that his entire life had been training for this walk. He would make it.

Inshallah.

He slung the bag of triggers over his shoulder and strode north through the desert, determined. He never saw the lion that took him.

64

"OK, what?" Ben asked bitterly while he opened his beer as directed.

"OK, so I am supposed to be in Johannesburg keeping our eyes on the triggers and setting up the inevitable bomb strike on the weapons factory in Iraq or Syria or wherever it is. Right now the CIA has no interest in you. Once you separated from the booty, you were no longer a factor. I had a job to do, and I figured you were resourceful enough to take care of yourself."

"And yet, here you sit."

"Right. It turns out that you have some sort of fairy godmother."

"That makes sense,".

"You really need to focus on the positive, dude. You are still breathing, and you have a beer in your hand."

"Seems pretty thin, Bob. What am I missing?"

"Well, I got an anonymous call at my house from a guy warning me to warn you. I traced the call to a pay phone in Maryland suspiciously close to Fort Meade. I think someone at the NSA is looking out for you."

"And so they called you at the CIA? Makes no sense."

"I think they called me not knowing that I was CIA. I think they called me because I am your friend, and if I traced it back right, I think this was the same guy who put Goodman on the case in the first place."

Ben was starting to get really fed up with this spy-versus-spy bullshit.

"OK, what did he say?" Ben asked, rubbing his forehead and hoping there would be a point coming along very soon.

"Well, what he said and I have since verified is that it looks like because this deal went sideways for Homeland Security, they are going to try and hang you for Goodman's murder to save face. Got an indictment written up, signed, and everything. Going for the death penalty."

Ben vomited a little into his mouth. He swallowed, thinking about the implications of that. It was a royal screwing, but he still had a moderately useful fake identity, and he was in Cape Town, which had a busy port. He doubted that they could track him to the New Zealand hinterlands. If he could still get there, his plan was still worth something.

"That it?" Ben asked.

"I am afraid not. FBI Hostage Rescue Team is on the ground in Cape Town and is working with the locals to bring you in, and as I understand it, they have been given a rather loose trigger policy on this one, the idea being that if you were killed during your apprehension, it would wrap everything up in a tidy bow and not expose the agencies involved to any further embarrassment in case you decided to testify at your trial."

"How much time have I got?"

Bob looked at his watch. "Best guess? Less than ten minutes."

"Take care of G-dog?"

"Of course."

Ben bolted from his chair, threw as much of his stuff as fast as he could into a bag, and zipped it up. He started for the door. Bob stopped him with an outstretched palm and a shaking head and said, "Window, dude."

"Thanks, man. I mean it. I'll send for Geronimo as soon as I land."

"Take your time."

Ben slid open the window carefully and slipped out behind the bushes. He could see them standing around in a group at the other end of the block. They were going through their last brief before approaching the cottage and hitting the door. Ben had done the same thing himself dozens of times when he was a fed. Quick talk with the locals who were now securing the perimeter and then blast the door. Bob was right: probably around ten minutes before the flash bang went into the room and blinded him. He saw Bob and Geronimo slink unnoticed out of the other window as the Cape Town PD was still setting up. They either didn't see Bob or knew it wasn't Ben; it looked like they got away clean. With every passing second, the noose was tightening. He had to come up with something. He could see his bashed-up Land Rover down the block. A very bored-looking local constable was responsible for watching Ben's car. That was his shot. He moved from shrub to shrub, getting as close to the car as he dared and as far away from his cottage as possible. He ended up behind a giant Bird of Paradise next to the sidewalk, about thirty meters from the house and about ten from the car. He waited.

65

It was a new guard who brought Karl Steiger his lunch as he sat in the federal prison building in downtown San Diego. He had his initial appearance before the judge this afternoon and was waiting on the US Marshalls to pick him up and walk him over to the courthouse. He was going to plead guilty to all of it. The conspiracy, the murders, everything. He was at peace. He smiled as he ate his baloney sandwich and drank his orange juice in one go. He finished his lunch and leaned back against the wall. The poison worked quickly. Karl soon realized he couldn't move. He slumped over sideways on the bunk, paralyzed. His mind still had a few moments of lucidity as he figured out what had happened. His mouth twisted sideways in a stroked-out half-smile as he closed his eyes and welcomed oblivion.

66

As soon as the concussion of the flash bang hit the cottage, Ben went mobile and blasted into the back of the poor street cop watching his car. The guy never had a chance. Ben slammed him into the Land Rover hard and then threw him to the ground, unconscious and in his own handcuffs, within ten seconds. True to form, the rest of the cops were watching the entry team and not the perimeter that was their task. Everyone always wanted to see the action. Ben figured they would have his small house cleared successfully in less than sixty seconds. He had to hit the road. He rolled the cop out of the street and onto the sidewalk so he wouldn't run him over and jumped in the car. Turning the ignition, the war-weary Rover cranked slowly, protesting. Ben prayed to the car gods for this thing to start. With every sad crank, Ben could see the patrol cops on the corners start to look around. It wouldn't take long to realize which car was starting and that they were one man short.

One of the guys on the corner about fifty yards away was pointing at Ben and speaking into his radio. Ben held the key down and looked over his shoulder as the FBI's vaunted Hostage Rescue Team started to filter out of the little house down the street. He could see their postures change as they received the radio communications. The diesel clattered to life, and Ben slammed down the gas pedal, pushing the car in front of him out of the way and racing off down the street. In his rearview mirror, Ben watched as uniforms scattered everywhere to separate vehicles to start the chase. He knew he didn't have a lot of options at this point; it was moment-to-moment survival. New intermediate goal: escape Cape Town. There would be safety in the bush if he could just get out of town and regroup. Ben had a vague knowledge of the layout of the city, and if he bolted north, he could get out.

Flat out the Rover flew, rattling along but somehow still mobile. He ran along the coast, occasionally spotting the blue lights behind him. He had a good lead. Over his left shoulder, he spotted Robben Island in the distance. He thought of Mandela and his long years there and shuddered, knowing that he was looking down the barrel of a similar fate. It felt like hours but was likely only ten minutes before he spotted the roadblock about a half mile down the road. North was out. No problem. East worked. Ben hung a right at a sign indicating Bloubergstrand and ducked into what appeared to be a middle-class neighborhood. Ben noticed that it had far lower walls and less razor wire than most of the neighborhoods he had seen in Johannesburg. It had small streets with short blocks and lots of cover, which was nice, but he had no idea where he was going. He could very easily have ended up at a dead end, on foot, hiding in someone's house in some sort of hostage situation. That would be checkmate. No winning there. He had to keep moving.

He picked his way through the neighborhood, heading east, his Defender spewing more white smoke by the minute out of the tailpipe. He eventually came to a road heading north to south with no more option for east. There were houses along the road and what appeared to be some sort of river valley beyond. He was boxed in. South it was. At least it would confuse his followers. Ben pulled over and took a breath. He tried to imagine what the map of Cape Town looked like. Sadly, the only things he really knew were the surf spots. He could see Table Mountain toward the south and had an idea. If he could make it there, there was enough wilderness for him to hide for a few days on foot. After that, he could still try to get on a boat and get out of there. Deep down, Ben knew they would be watching the port if he got away, but one step at a time.

Just as he was about to roll off, he saw another Defender just like his turn the corner behind him. He could see that the car had at least four occupants all armed with long guns. It even had the Bear Claw logo on the door. Ben slouched. This was not happening. The Bear Claw Land Rover approached slowly and cautiously. Ben wasn't running, and they were confused. Ben press-checked his pistol, put the car in reverse, and floored it, emptying the magazine through the rear window. He put at least three where the driver's head should have been, but behind the shattered glass, he couldn't be sure if they connected. The vehicles definitely did. He impacted the front of their car demolition-derby style, full speed in reverse. He felt his neck rip sideways from the impact. Several bursts of wild gunfire shot straight up through the roof from the impact. Idiots with their fingers on the triggers. Ben slowly and painfully cranked his neck around forward and put the car in first. He peeled away from the Bear Claw truck, which was now spilling water from underneath the front. If Ben could get a block or two away, they were out of the game. His car wheezed along. In his mirror he saw several disorientated mercs spill out of the now defunct Rover and throw a few rounds his way. Ben turned down a street, now west and out of the line of fire. Ben liked his new Table Mountain wilderness idea. It was simple, didn't require anything special. He just had to get there.

He found the main highway south. Nobody was on him yet. This was good. He would try to be as inconspicuous as he could, dump the rig, and hide out for a while. He got the truck up to fifty miles per hour on the expressway, a respectable speed provided you could get past the missing windows, bullet holes, and white smoke pouring out the back. Ben reached down and turned on the radio. "Gimme Shelter" came out through the remaining functioning speaker, some sort of rare concert version. Ben smiled. He liked this song, and it definitely was appropriate for today. He could see the mountains of the Cape getting closer, and he could feel himself going feral. The Cape Town Metropolitan Police Opel Astra came quickly up the on-ramp behind him. It took only a few moments of radio chatter for the blue lights to come on. Ben floored it again. More and more cars joined the chase. It had the feel of midnineties Los Angeles. Trade the Land Rover for a white Ford Bronco, and you were there. Table Mountain was on his right; he would need to exit to get there, but the freeway just kept going. Ben had a vague notion that most of the mountainous area of the Cape was undeveloped; he just had to find a window. He kept going as fast as he could, his truck hitting seventy. He was running out of land. He knew that if he got to a stop and jumped out, the police were close enough to just mow him down as he ran. He needed some distance or a new plan. After a minute he got one.

67

The Opel Astras of the Cape Town Metropolitan Police had no problem keeping up with the bullet-ridden Land Rover. The cops at the wheel rightly assumed the vehicle was not long for this world and that they could just scoop up Ben Adams as soon as he wheeled to a stop. Via radio they also knew that the FBI HRT was en route, and they were under orders to take "no unnecessary action" until the FBI got there, whatever the hell that meant. It was a Yankee problem, probably best sorted out by the Yankees themselves, so they followed closely and waited.

Ben was humming past Table Mountain and into Hout Bay, where he could see a fogbank lined up against the coast. This was good. Ben knew there was a marina and beach there, and they were critical to his amended plan. Back in Cape Town proper, Ben had been surrounded by roads and city infrastructure, which meant the people who were after him would be able to tighten the knot with their radios until they inevitably captured or killed him. Once he got to Hout Bay, the tables would turn a little bit. The town was surrounded by mountains and water, with only one valley leading in or out. This kept everybody on one side of Ben, and he could theoretically escape if he could just get a couple of minutes to get away. Ripping into the village as fast as his now rapidly dying transport would take him, he swung left onto Northshore Drive. The name sounded about right, and it was pointed the right way, so he took it. As he rapidly approached the end of the road, he saw the beach straight ahead and the marina to his right.

He had to make a quick judgment call. He went totally straight. Full throttle, he jumped over the sand dunes at the edge of the beach and onto the sand. Miraculously, the Land Rover kept going, tires spinning the sand in big fantails. He pushed straight through and into the water. The white beast didn't finally stop until the ocean was past the former windshield. Ben undid his seat belt and crawled out through the windshield frame. He stood on the hood and surveyed his surroundings. The cops were hung up on the dunes and were out of their cars, confused and on their radios trying to figure out what to do. One or two of the more aggressive ones were working their way down the beach toward Ben on foot, although it was unclear if they were willing to swim for him. Ben released the straps holding his tattered blue surfboard on the roof.

Paddle away. Easy enough. Get into the fog; come ashore later somewhere else.

He tied his wetsuit around his neck. The water was cold. He would get into it as soon as he was safely hidden in the fog. He strapped his leash to his foot and paddled off into the calm waters of Hout Bay. He could feel the occasional bulge of a swell pass beneath him, suggesting what the ocean was doing outside of the protected waters of the bay. He heard faint shouting from the shoreline as the first wisps of fog touched his skin. A few hundred yards more and he would be hidden from view. After about a quarter of a mile of hard paddling, Ben stopped to catch his breath. He sat up on his board. It would be only a matter of time before the fog lifted and the boats and helicopters came for him. The good news was that he was in his element. At this point, Ben felt nowhere more at home than in the ocean and on a surfboard.

He started to shiver, remembering that the water was in the midfifties, the cold Benguela Current keeping the water chilly and full of nutrients for a robust food chain that Ben was now swimming in. With the sun obscured by the fog, he was getting cold quickly. He unleashed his board and wiggled into his wetsuit—definitely a challenge in the water, but he did it quickly. As soon as he got his wetsuit zipped up, he heard a faint booming sound. Surely they couldn't be bombing him? It was too far away. Mining? It sounded like it was coming off the water. The fog could be playing tricks on him. Another boom. Ben slowly put it together. Dungeons. He visualized the road map of the Cape in his head, and he matched it with what he remembered of the surf map from his flight over. Hout Bay was the put-in point for a trip to Dungeons, that nightmare of a surf spot he had read about. It was a mile away over deep water, literally teeming with great whites. In fact, tour-boat operators in the area routinely chummed the waters so deep-pocketed morons could get into a cage in the water with giant predators who were now associating humans with food.

The odds were still with him, he thought. Killed by a great white today? Probably not. Worst case, still sounds better than jail or getting shot by the same FBI that had already ruined his life once. Maybe there were other surfers out there whom Ben could blend in with, maybe jump in a boat with and ride back, slipping by unnoticed. Given Ben's current slate of options, that one sounded pretty good. He started paddling toward the sound. He was in good enough shape that a mile paddle over rough water wouldn't be too big of a deal. He was fairly well destroyed after the last few days, but he lived in the water; he could make this paddle right off the couch after a hard night of drinking at the West End.

Boom. Louder this time. He was starting to feel the impact through his surfboard. He kept stroking.

Occasionally he would stop, catch his breath, and listen. It had to be big. Ben didn't know enough about the spot to know if it even broke at a small size, but based on the acoustics alone, it was macking. A few more minutes and Ben had to slow down. He couldn't see the land and hadn't heard a wave in a while. He definitely did not want to get caught inside here. Something boiled to the left of him. Water off the reef? Kelp moving in the current? Large toothy fish? He pulled his feet up onto his board and waited for a moment. Nothing. He relaxed a bit and let his feet back into the water. What was he protecting at this point? He felt it before he heard it: another big impact followed by a sound Ben could compare only to an F-18 at full tilt ripping over his head, common enough in San Diego. This was no F-18; it was the wave, and even though he still couldn't see it, he knew he was close. The white water from the impact of the last wave came roiling by in a way that created thousands of tiny drops of water that bounced on the surface of the ocean among the foam. Ben had seen it only a few times before in his life. He marveled at the little spheres dancing around him and watched the light play and sparkle. Sparkle? Ben looked up and noticed that the fog was starting to break up.

Shit.

Maybe not. Maybe it was good news. Maybe he could find his way into the lineup easier and blend in with the other guys if there was sun. Ben just tried to stay where he was and wait for the sky to clear. He could feel himself being pulled toward the wave as it approached. A pulse of energy that big draws lots of water off the reef. He thought that meant he was in front of the wave. Not good. He would have to paddle around. He started easily paddling at a forty-five-degree angle to where he thought the wave was. This would hopefully put him on the shoulder where he could paddle behind to the peak. The fog dissipated quickly and revealed a starkly beautiful day with maybe an hour or two of sunlight left. Ben closed his eyes and faced the sun, letting it warm his skin and the blackness of his wetsuit. After a moment, he opened his eyes and could see the foam from waves that had already broken. Assuming the current hadn't dragged the foam too far, he was indeed on the shoulder, presumably safe. The horizon started to rise, end to end; the whole world looked like it was about to flip. Ben paddled hard toward the bulge. When it finally broke, he was outside the impact zone, but he had to crawl straight up the surge, looking over his shoulder into the barrel of what had to be a fifty-foot wave.

He was mesmerized. It was perfect. No wind. Not a drop out of place. A dream wave on a nightmare scale. He took a few more strokes to make sure he was on the right side of the next one. He looked around. There was nobody there. Surely a wave this big and this good would have some of the locals on it. Maybe they knew something he didn't. Maybe it wasn't worth coming out in the fog. Looking back to shore, he could see the fog breaking up there as well. Within fifteen minutes, the coast would be clear, and hopefully the waves would be visible from shore. Surely surfers would come then. Ben stroked a little closer to what he believed was the lineup. Another wave was coming. He forced down the paranoia that the ocean was going to eat him and stayed put. He was fairly certain he was safe. The swell started pulling him up the face, and as he went straight up, he could feel the kinetic energy start to fold over. At the top, he realized he was right: at least fifty feet. He was five stories off the ocean and seemingly dead even with the mountains on shore. The same horrendous jet sounds as this one detonated on the reef. He stayed where he was. Every few minutes another one came through, and his adrenaline spiked. He inched closer to the takeoff zone. In big-wave surfing, it isn't really the surfing skill that you need; it is the survival skill to navigate the waves and get out of a wipeout alive that really defines the big-wave surfer, not to mention the courage to try it in the first place. Ben was not that guy; he was a good surfer and happy enough to charge the big winter days in San Diego. No slouch, to be sure, but this was something else. This was the type of spot for the craziest of the crazy hellmen. People who don't mind San Francisco's Ocean Beach in midwinter. Guys who will spend hours in the water hoping for the stars to align so they can get one wave. These were the guys who Ben was hoping were on their way with their boats so he could get the fuck out of there. Yet he inched closer.

After about thirty minutes, the coast was entirely clear of fog. Ben was alone, and the surf was cranking in a way that was scarcely believable. As in it was hard to accept that it was real. It was as if he were on some sort of beautiful and terrifying acid trip where the physics governing water no longer applied. He knew that based on his fitness, age, and skill, for him to take off on one of these waves was not exactly certain death but definitely likely death. Should he wipe out, there would be no one to zoom in on a Jet Ski and save him from the next impact. He would take a set of fifty-footers on the head, likely to his doom. He didn't have the capacity to survive a three-wave hold-down. He should call it a day, turn around, paddle in, and deal with whatever awaited him on shore. Yet closer he went. He kept telling himself that he just wanted to see it a little better, get a better feel for it in case someday he came back and wanted to surf it. The delusions were stacking up quickly. He was having a hard time maintaining the dissonance. The next big wave came through, and Ben rode the surge to the top, craning his head back toward shore. Two boats rounding the headland from the marina at Houts Bay. He saw a blue light glint off one of them.

Police.

Maybe not. Maybe just a blue surfboard sitting in the nose of an open-bow Boston Whaler? The local crew coming out to get some of this bounty? Definitely. Standard surf deal, not the police or the FBI. That made more sense. Ben noticed the next wave starting its march skyward. He stared at it as it thundered toward him. He could feel the wind getting pushed by the surge. This one was bigger than the others. He felt the wave start to draw him toward it. He was in the right spot for a larger wave breaking just a bit farther out on the reef. It would be there in less than thirty seconds. The boat was at least two minutes out. He was in the perfect spot. For a sixty-foot wave. Injured, close to sunset, and all alone. He had to touch the stove. He turned and paddled hard for it. He felt the surge beneath him as he gained speed. The ocean in front of him dropped away as the wave built beneath him. His head down, arms churning, the wave started to push him as it feathered at the top. He jumped to his feet in a crouch and accelerated down the giant face of the wave.

ACKNOWLEDGMENTS

The idea for this book came from several high profile cases of krytron smuggling, and my time in South Africa in 2010. The remainder of the story and the characters are completely fictional. My descriptions of the locations in this book stem entirely from affection, and I encourage readers to visit all of them. Thanks to everyone who has supported my writing habit by buying and/or reading my first two books. Also, thanks to Karyn DeConcini, Clark Settles, Peter Gelfan, Ross Browne, Sue Doucette and Robert Blake Whitehill, your help and support over the years has been priceless. Also, thanks to CreateSpace for making such a great platform, it has truly changed my life. All mistakes and offenses are mine alone.

For information on the Baja Dog Rescue, please go to www.bajadogrescue.org and get yourself a new friend like Geronimo!

79446895R10178

Made in the USA
Columbia, SC
01 November 2017